The Sara Chronicles Book One

We Were Destined

Laura Hughes

Dedicated to God, David and Sara

Into every life some trouble must come. But what happens when trouble is all you know and learning to survive is just a matter of routine? This is the beginning of a story in which struggle builds character and love is something that has to be awoken after a long sleep... And so this is Sara's story...

Chapter One

Someone made a terrible mistake twelve years ago, placing a homeless child in the care of Janet and Hugh Finklestein. This child's life was proof that a higher power does indeed look out for the helpless innocents of this world. Small and vulnerable, this tender life was entrusted to callus, heartless souls who cared for her with less compassion than they might bestow upon an unwanted family pet. Though the Finklesteins were wealthy by the standards of the day, this child didn't benefit from their prosperity. Her life was one of poverty under a luxurious roof. They did little to make things pleasant for this small child. She wasn't really theirs, after all. And yet, despite the neglect, the misplaced orphan never got sick or starved. She continued to grow and thrive as if nourishment and care were provided from somewhere deep within.

Whatever her fortification, it kept her alive, even among a hostile family who didn't even bother to give her a name. But a name wasn't necessary. She came with one preprogrammed into her soul with an understanding that she would know it when she needed to. In fact, she told them to call her Sara when she was able speak, frightening them with the certainty of her own identity.

At this point in their relationship, both parties knew little about the reason for her being with them beyond their duty to see that she be kept alive. But being alive was far different from being happy, loved and secure in a continued existence. But little did she know, the Finklesteins were afraid to let her die. Not for reasons the average person might understand, more a self-preserving impulse than a moral or ethical one. For whatever reason, her survival, as miserable as it was, was necessary for their own. That Sara grew to be a remarkable young girl, despite the minimal attention given her, was a downright miracle.

She was a well-mannered, sweet child, well-thought-of by all who knew her. But the trouble was: no one really knew her. Self-contained, solitary, Sara occupied space in a world of terrifying strangers. This girl possessed unique characteristics, an inner glow that made her stand out in a crowd. She seemed strangely complete inside, like she was carrying more beneath her skin than was immediately apparent. And while the Finklestein family despised her, she had a different effect on the rest of the world. She made an impression that had people staring as she walked across a room. She carried herself well, shoulders straight, with perfect posture. In some cases, too careful, like she was walking on eggshells, as if afraid to become too attached to people and places she might have to abandon at a moment's notice. In conversation, she spoke slowly, to avoid saying the wrong thing, and never made eye contact, even when speaking directly to someone.

Though never seeking out others, many people wanted to be near her. When she began to attend school, children were drawn to Sara like moths to a flame – a flame she quickly learned to dim until she was almost as invisible as she wished to be. The remarkable girl they remembered vanished into an ordinariness of her own choosing, until most weren't even sure they'd met her at all. It was safer that way.

There was always an underlying fear in her, a little rabbit in a world of ravenous wolves. For many years, Sara commuted from school to the fairy tale mansion where her time was spent in total misery. Day after day, she plodded through life trying to avoid being noticed by her adoptive family, because if they ignored her, the verbal abuse would not come. She would not be called the skinny little ingrate, the terrible mistake. If they just ignored her, she would not be berated for every action and thought she'd ever had.

There would be no problems if she just became so small they didn't notice her. *Please don't notice me. Please don't punish me. I'll be like a little mouse. I don't like the dark room. I don't like being made to sit and go hungry while I watch you eat. Please just pretend that I'm not here at all.* But inside, the young girl had a tremendously strong will, which kept her going day after day. She played their game, listened with one ear, making herself as invisible as possible, always feeling there was something beyond life with the Finklesteins. Though high on the social ladder, the couple was low on the moral ladder. They would lie, cheat, and steal, while conducting themselves in public as if they had no idea what the word dishonest meant. Like poisonous chameleons, these people who called themselves her parents blended into their surroundings, winning the trust of those around them. No one would ever suspect that Hugh Finklestein was the mastermind of many a shady land deal, selling non-existent parcels of land to unsuspecting buyers, that he used stolen credit cards, sold fake identities to questionable characters, and may or may not have engineered robberies with a gang of small-time thugs. Janet was just as bad; her internet sales of low quality and illegally obtained products earned them millions of dollars. They had moved many a time to remain ahead of the long arm of the law; because Hugh was very good at covering their tracks, hiding behind many false businesses and sometimes changing their names altogether. In fact, Finklestein, though it was the only identity she could remember, may not have been their real names. Sara accompanied them on all the wild flights from place to place. They didn't want her but seemed afraid to let her go, even though she was told daily that she was not their biological child.

It was obvious that these dark, burly people with thick noses and even thicker foreheads had not sired a little blonde girl with a perfect oval face, wide eyes and straight thin nose that turned up slightly at the end. While her step-siblings were well-fed, Sara was very thin, almost painfully so. Most people said that a good meal had passed her by many a time. Pale skin desperately in need of a little sunshine was accentuated by bright blue eyes that carried a sad, faraway look. She knew she belonged somewhere else. The Finklesteins were, to say it kindly, not very attractive people and not just in matter of appearance; they were ugly in the way that they acted towards others. Janet and Hugh, not Mom and Dad, were kind only in the regard of furthering their livelihoods. They were quite the benefactors, donating generously to the local school and other local charities. Throughout the years, they had learned something quite interesting – acting rich attracted other rich people. And knowing rich people was very good for business. They would seek out and cultivate the most influential citizens of the town and *help* them to make investments. These investments would sometimes pay off a little, and helped maintain a degree of legitimacy. Most of the money went into their pockets but they could explain away the losses by saying that investments were risky. People tended to accept that as a well-known truth. "Got to be careful," Hugh would say. "Don't mess with anyone too close to home. That's how you get caught. I'm too smart to get caught." Then he and Janet would laugh about how there was a sucker born every minute, you just had to have the skill to spot them.

The Finklesteins liked the little town of Midland and planned to stay awhile, so they kept their business affairs mostly long-distance and low-key. Their children, Amy and Andy, were horribly spoiled and selfish.

They had all the latest gadgets: cell phones with every imaginable feature, laptop computers, expensive entertainment centers in each of their rooms. Yet they had nothing: no character, no kindness, no love for anyone other than themselves. The two children were mean to Sara because their parents were. It was an accepted fact that she just wasn't part of their real family. She was just there because…well, they weren't sure why she was there. Amy had asked her parents once why they had brought this child home ten years ago. Her mother had looked her right in the eye and said that they couldn't really avoid taking the girl in. "Money's money no matter where it comes from." She'd said and would explain no more, soothing her children with kisses, candy, and gifts to ease her conscience.

When she first arrived, the children, not yet having been corrupted by hate, tried to provide some comfort. They soon learned that their parents did not like this at all. Amy and Andy were strongly discouraged from showing any kindness to Sara. They now felt perfectly comfortable with calling her all kinds of names and giving her their chores to do. In time, they ignored her altogether; the stupid girl didn't even fight back. Sadly, in addition to having lost their compassion, Amy and Andy had lost their will to do anything constructive for themselves. They were beyond overweight, massive frames straining at the seams of their designer jeans, providing an interesting contrast to Sara's emaciated body. Each of their plump faces were blighted with shiny pustules that could easily be solved by proper diet and exercise, but most likely never would. Any friends the pair had were a result of their parents' wealth. At such a young age, Amy and Andy were set on a tragic path, one they might never stray from as they had no other examples to follow.

While Amy and Andy's every need was attended to, Sara learned to work to obtain the things she needed. All her possessions were bought with money earned from a paper route she'd arranged for herself. The young girl saved all her pay, going regularly to the thrift shops on Huntington Avenue. It was at these places that the owners allowed her to purchase entire bags of used clothing for ridiculously low prices. She was always so polite and thankful. The shopkeepers went out of their way to find her the nicest things in her size and set them aside for her. The owners thought so highly of the girl, they would have given them to her free, but Sara insisted on paying; it was the right thing to do. She knew somewhere inside that she had to do her best, no matter what happened – it was expected by… the answer to that dangling question evaded her. Maybe it was the feminine voice in her head she had come to call her conscience. *Don't be like them* the voice said to her on more than one occasion. *You are meant for better* was another of the messages that came through in the silent time just before sleep overtook her. She wanted to ask the voice why she was here and why it didn't love her enough to help her leave, but it didn't work that way. There was no predictable pattern to the messages she would receive and what she heard didn't always immediately make sense. The silence would stretch out for long periods only to re-emerge when she felt control had left and she couldn't endure another moment of life as it was.

That something that shared her mind chose not to relieve her suffering only to keep her alive. Knowing only that she couldn't give up, the resourceful girl even managed to stash some groceries in her bedroom so that she would not starve. Mostly fruit, chips, and canned meats. Not the best of diets, but any food was better than no food at all. *Survive*, the message played in her head over and over, so she listened and continued on as best as she could. This thought carried her through days when she didn't think she could endure another second in this place. Day after day, she got up early, delivered her papers, and continued to attend school because somehow it was all very important, she just didn't know why. School was Sara's saving grace. The Finklestein's allowed her to go because it was against the law to forbid it. Try as they might to deny her, she was a registered member of their family in the eyes of the law. Others were aware she existed and it was necessary to go through the motions of normalcy. Sara loved school and excelled in all her classes. This was of no comfort to Janet, who had to poke and prod Amy and Andy to attend. If they made a D+ on their report cards, it was an occasion to celebrate. To Sara, school was a welcome escape from the negative atmosphere of home. Her teachers praised her efforts and encouraged her to participate in extra-curricular activities. This, of course, was not welcomed with a positive response from Janet. The answer was no. "Sara has too much to do at home." she had said when asked. But it had given Janet an idea. If Sara was doing so well in school, maybe she could use it to her advantage. It was around that time that Amy and Andy's grades had drastically improved.

It was not that they were putting in any effort, it was because Sara was now doing all their schoolwork. To try and keep up, Sara began doing homework from the minute that she arrived home from her paper deliveries. She was still doing homework until about eleven o'clock each evening, and that was on a good day when she didn't have to familiarize herself with new information (Amy and Andy were two and three grades ahead of her – and had been for several years). Maybe this year they would pass on to the next grade.

For the fourth time that week, the family went out to dinner without Sara. Seeing this as a welcome respite, Sara sat at home completing a report on scientific advances in health care for Amy to turn in. The small girl sat in her dimly lit basement room, shivering from the cold, pulling her sweater closer about her thin frame as she tried to concentrate on what she was reading. In contrast to the luxury home above her this was the slum section, yet she tried to make it homely. Sara had purchased a few heavy quilts from the thrift store to keep her small bed warm. The bare concrete floor had a few brightly colored rag rugs scattered here and there, and two small space heaters kept some of the chill away. Pictures of smiling family groups torn from magazines graced the walls; families she liked to pretend were her own. This was her refuge. Thankfully, the Finklesteins would not go beyond the basement steps; they considered it a nasty, filthy place that they were too good to enter and she was very grateful for that.

Sara sat at her small desk made from cinder blocks and a plank of wood painstakingly poring over the information in front of her. She was very tired and had to read the paper carefully because the words were beginning to blur. Struggling to stay awake, Sara finished the last sentence, walked up three flights of stairs with heavy legs, and laid it on Amy's dresser. The sounds of the girl's snores serenaded her on the trip back downstairs. Then, using her last bit of strength, she walked back to the basement, collapsed on her cot, and fell fast asleep.

Chapter Two

A new day began to the soft ringing of her alarm clock. Rubbing eyes still swollen from far too little sleep, Sara stumbled out of bed and dressed for school. Hoping to stave off the cold, she put her warmest sweater on, chose a thick pair of black pants and her heavy black jacket. Studying herself carefully in the cracked mirror she'd obtained from a dumpster down the street, Sara ran a comb through her hair and nodded in satisfaction. She wanted to look nice today for her favorite teacher Mrs. Swan.

Mrs. Swan had promised to treat her to breakfast that morning if she was able to be at school by 6:30. Sara was looking forward to attending. Breakfast was a rare treat, and she loved to talk to her English teacher. Mrs. Swan would often loan Sara books from her home library, books that she treated with the greatest of care. Rather than go to recess like the other children, Sara would stay in Mrs. Swan's classroom talking about classics such as *The Hobbit*, *Great Expectations*, and *The Great Gatsby*, with an understanding of literature that surprised and delighted her teacher. Mrs. Swan was the closest thing she had to a friend, the one person she hadn't withdrawn from completely.

With a small sigh, she acknowledged to herself that this might have to change someday. It wouldn't do to become too attached to this world, to one person like that, but it wouldn't be today. Today she was going to enjoy the small pleasure of being important to someone.

As she gingerly opened the basement door, Sara was aware that Janet would try to stop her if she knew she was going, not out of concern for the early hour, but out of general spite at her eagerness to go. The house was thankfully silent; none of the other occupants seemed to be awake and about. She crossed carefully through the large kitchen and out the side door unnoticed, wincing as her feet made crunching noises on the stone step outside, relaxing only when she closed the door and felt safe. Reaching behind the trash cans at the side of the house, Sara lifted out the heavy canvas bag the local paper vendor left there for her every morning. She then walked four miles to school, tossing newspapers into doorways as she passed her customer's homes. Her breath made billowy clouds in the air as she walked; her boot heels little clicking noises on the frozen concrete surface in the otherwise still morning. The crisp air made her face feel tight and her chest hurt but she felt surprisingly good. She was, after all, going to do something she enjoyed with someone she adored and that was worth braving the weather and early start.

The sun was just coming up when she reached the school. Rushing to a small side door she knew would be unlocked, Sara entered the warm building. She spent a wonderful hour with Mrs. Swan discussing the latest book she had read and paper that she was writing for the essay contest. As they ate delicious blueberry pancakes, Mrs. Swan steered the conversation to Sara's home life. This was something her teacher often did when they had the chance to talk and, though she appreciated the concern, she knew it was a sign that their friendship would have to end soon. She would have to blend in to the background again, avoiding even this small comfort. It was the unfortunate reality of her life. It would never do to have anyone get involved in her personal misery. It would not end well for them. Among other things, her inner voice had made this understood in a thousand vague ways – her situation should be hers alone.

This, therefore, would have to be the last good day they had together. Sara looked at her teacher sadly and carefully avoided the questions about how much she'd had to eat, was she getting enough sleep and how was the family treating her. She was aware that Mrs. Swan had made several trips to the principal's office on her behalf to try to get him to investigate the Finklesteins treatment of her. She had been so many times that Mr. Beals had finally threatened to fire her if she showed up again. He did not want to do anything to offend the Finklesteins for fear that they might withdraw funding for the new indoor track and other projects they had promised to help with. Sara could not have this happen to Mrs. Swan, so she went out of her way to avoid any further questions and was very careful not to make any comments that would cause the teacher to visit the principal again.

Still Mrs. Swan did her best to discover something she could use to remove Sara from what she suspected was a very bad situation. But Sara did not give her the chance, diverting her attention by asking her about a book she wanted to borrow. As Mrs. Swan went to get the book, Sara silently said goodbye to her beloved teacher and walked out to the now crowded hallway.

Joining the herd of students moving along the corridor, Sara entered a classroom and spent the rest of the day completing mid-semester exams. Concentrating on the work at hand gave Sara little time to think about losing her only connection to this world. But as the end of the school day approached, she grew more anxious. Pushing back sadness and fear, she heard the last bell and moved out to join the crowd of kids escaping for the afternoon. Large groups of students walked past as she made her way down the long hallway towards her locker. She passed a bulletin board with a sign proclaiming that homecoming was just around the corner and elections for the king and queen were to be held next week. Kids her age were talking on cell phones and making plans for the weekend. And here she was in the middle of it all. The world was going on around her and she was completely alone. These kids had friends, families, and things to do; she had hatred and loneliness.

And this was Friday. And above all, she hated Fridays. Sara dreaded going home because she knew it would be two days before she could come back. Two whole days, which she would have to spend at home doing endless chores and putting up with the constant verbal abuse the Finklesteins handed out. Resigned to her fate, Sara slowly walked home, the feeling of dread growing with each step. Her trip home took twice as long; she was in no hurry to reach her destination. Maybe if she took her time, the family would be out to dinner or one of the other events they were known to attend most evenings. Time had taught her to minimize her misery by avoiding contact with the Finklesteins. It didn't always work. But when it did it was wonderful.

Only today, the closer she got to the house, the worse she felt. A knot in her stomach, Sara's steps faltered. Her mouth became dry. The voice in her head was mumbling incoherently, sending out urgent messages she could not decipher. It had never done that before. But as it wasn't offering her anything certain to work with, Sara didn't see how she could avoid returning to the house.

Looking down at her hands, she was distressed to see them shaking when she stashed her canvas bag in its usual hiding-place at the side of the house and prepared her entry strategy. There was no turning back from her path now. She was almost home and there was nowhere else to go. All the cars were parked in the driveway. Maybe if she could just sneak through the kitchen and get to her room without them seeing, she could stay down there until they left. Taking a deep breath, Sara grasped the knob and slowly turned it. Her hopes for an undetected entry were quickly dashed. As soon as her foot crossed the threshold she was pulled inside by Janet and Amy.

"What did you think you were doing?" yelled Amy. "How dare you mess up my report! You deliberately sabotaged me!"

Puzzled by the ambush, Sara stared open-mouthed at Janet and Amy. Both were practically foaming at the mouth with anger. Highly polished talon-like nails gripped stick thin arms and Janet pushed Sara backward. The heavy-set woman was waving her arms wildly, causing Sara to duck and step back to avoid contact while looking for a way to defuse the situation. But the screaming attack continued as she attempted to get her bearings and figure out what was going on. Thin sheets of paper were flung at her face. Sara managed to grasp a page with shaking fingers, quickly recognizing a few lines she had written early this morning before leaving them in Amy's room.

"She got an F on her paper." Janet raged. "Do you think that was funny?"

"I don't understand," Sara said timidly. "I did what you asked; I wrote the paper,"

"Well, you didn't finish it." Amy wailed. "It started out so good, then it just ended with a bunch of scribbled words. The teacher was going to let me finish it on break, but I didn't know what to write, so she gave me an F!"

"I must have been so tired that I didn't notice the mistake," Sara said.

"Well, I've had enough of you and your excuses, young lady!" Janet yelled. "Get to your room. We'll decide what to do with you later!" With that, Janet shoved Sara to the basement door and pushed her inside.

The next thing Sara knew, she was falling down the stairs.

Chapter Three

Sara was falling onto a pile of soft grass. Grass? She felt the ground underneath her. How could this be? Instead of the hard, concrete floor, Sara was lying in a field of fresh grass, could feel the silky blades brush her fingertips, smell the verdant foliage surrounding her. When she looked up, Sara could see a beautiful, clear night sky full of stars. Shocked by the sudden change in her location, she began to frantically touch her head, searching for signs of wounds which would indicate the nature of injury that must be causing her to hallucinate so badly. She didn't feel any lumps or bumps. Surprisingly, her head didn't hurt in the least; in fact, she felt better now than she had in a long time. *Hey, I'm free!* she thought excitedly. *I'm no longer in that horrible place!*

Elated by her sudden freedom, she got up and danced a little jig of joy, leaping, and tumbling about like a silly toddler. When she was too tired to continue, she gathered her composure and looked more carefully at her surroundings. The night sky was alight with a beautiful full moon illuminating the landscape, making everything more brilliant and clear. The grass glowed with a vibrant green color; the dew sticking to the blades shone from the ground like sparkling diamonds lying loosely in the soil. Clumps of yellow flowers throughout the field cast a shadow on the grass next to it, which was strange to see at night. The moonlight was so bright it sparkled as brightly as the sun. The dark sky glowed like soft velvet, wrapping around her, making her feel so comfortable, so much at home. And this was something new because home, in its purest sense, had always been a place she had never known.

The field was large and empty except for her and a few trees scattered every few feet. No structures were visible, not even in the distance. The only sounds to be heard were the distant chirping of some crickets and the occasional hooting of an owl. Sara didn't mind being here by herself; she found the isolation peaceful. At last, she was safe and secure. And it felt wonderful.

Despite her enjoyment of the moment, it eventually occurred to Sara that maybe she should try out and find out exactly where she was and why she was here. Drawing in a deep breath to steady her nerves, she began to walk towards some of the trees in hope that she would soon come to a road, house, some sign of civilization. Walking for what seemed to be an awfully long time, the girl wandered toward the only objects visible on the landscape: the trees.

The trees were her main point of focus as she crossed the field. But once she neared them, they seemed to multiply from a sparsely wooded area to a thick forest. There wasn't much transition from flat open land to dark, gloomy woodland. One minute there was grass and visible sky above her, a few steps later there was little light visible between the top most branches. Slender trails led between the trees; indistinct paths winding to nowhere causing the sole wanderer to stop and stare around her indecisively.

A slight noise. The snapping of twigs and muffled voices swam faintly in the air, causing the young girl to peer cautiously around her. Sara looked into the thickest clump of trees and saw a faint glow coming from the center. Reminding herself that she had come this way in search of people, she started to move cautiously toward the light. Tiptoeing softly into the trees, she could now see that the light came from a campfire, and that two people were sitting facing each other across from the flames. The two people, a man and woman, were talking too softly for her to hear, so she moved closer, picking her way carefully through dead branches littering the forest floor. Footstep after careful footstep carried her closer to a tree just a few feet from the fire. Hand braced against the tree, trying not to breathe too heavily and give herself away, Sara strained to listen in. The pair looked harmless, but she couldn't be sure. If she could only hear what they were saying. Leaning forward as far as she dared, she tried to remain unseen, but the woman turned suddenly and looked directly at her. "Come on then, dear," she said, gesturing Sara forward with her hand. "We've been waiting for you for some time. Please, don't be shy."

Sara looked at the woman in amazement, and couldn't shake the feeling that the woman really had been expecting her. She was small, with a pleasant face and wild orange hair that stuck out of her thin head at all angles. The brightest green eyes Sara had ever seen glittered like emeralds from her kindly face. She sensed no danger, and eager to find out who this woman was, crept closer to the fire.

"Oh, please, do sit down, Sara," said the woman's companion.

He too appeared very happy to see her. As he spoke his large, round body shifted to look in her direction. Wisps of gray hair clung to a balding head that was smooth as a fresh tomato. Inquisitive eyes studied her with a pleasure reflected with the showing of pearly white teeth. He beckoned her forward with plump fingers twinkling with the adornment of many colorful rings- all the while continuing a conversation as if she should understand what he was talking about.

"We don't have much time to go over things with you. Goodness knows we had a devil of a time figuring out where you were. It seems that we got you out just in time. They were getting a little rough with you, weren't they? Well, it will all even out in time, I expect. What goes around comes around, you know." He patted the log on which he was sitting to encourage Sara to join him.

"How did you know my name?" she asked, stepping into the well-lit area without the normal hesitation of someone who'd just met some very strange strangers.

Though the woman's appearance was eye-catching and unique, this man was a big bundle of comforting fascination for her. Everything about him was somehow familiar. He had the oddest gray eyes, not unpleasant, just different in the best way – looking into them was like staring into a clear mountain stream, soothing and exhilarating at the same time. Unable to resist his friendly summons, Sara reached out her hand and allowed him to envelope it in his larger one.

"Oh, we know a lot about you, dear," he said, touching Sara's tiny white arm with his other hand, wincing sympathetically at the fragile feel of it. "Oh, my, you are thin. I expect they didn't spare much time or expense to care for you properly, did they?"

As Sara perched on the edge of the log, he reached back and pulled out the largest plate of food she had ever seen. There were piles of thinly sliced turkey, an enormous clump of bright purple grapes, deep red tomatoes, and sliced cheese so yellow that it looked like rays of sunshine had settled on the plate. Sara hesitated briefly before taking the plate and eating with trembling hands. She didn't want to appear rude, but she was awfully hungry and found herself picking up a grape daintily between her fingers when all she wanted to do was grab great handfuls of food. As soon as the thought left her mind, the man's smile became even brighter. Shaking her head to dismiss the idea that he had just read her thoughts, Sara picked up some cheese and turkey, combining them into a breadless sandwich which she began to eat heartily.

22

"That's right, dear, eat well. You will need your strength. I must apologize for the poor choice of caregivers. You see, we had to leave that task to others at the time. We thought it best not to know where you were in case something went wrong. My name is Ferd, and this is Maggie." He nodded towards the woman who also began to talk as if Sara should already be fully aware of the situation. The pair wasted little time, speaking as if every second was precious, not to be squandered on meaningless chit-chat. "Where am I?" Sara mumbled the necessary question, covering her mouth to hide the fact that she hadn't quiet swallowed her mouthful of food yet.

"The Land of the Keepers." Ferd answered in puzzled tones, as if he were stating another obvious fact she should already know.

"There is not much time for us here," Maggie said. "It's our task to help set you on your way. There are two others that you must find. Where they are exactly, we do not know. Together you will be powerful. You must set things right or we are all lost," she explained, a look of dread crossing her face.

"Wait a minute" Sara hadn't intended to interrupt but she couldn't help herself. "What do you mean, exactly?"

"Here, I have written a few things down that might help," said Ferd, almost apologetically, placing a folded piece of paper on the log next to her. "To find them, you must continue on the path through the woods. Do not stray from it. There are others who are anxious to find them, too. But you must get to them first. What you all seek is a symbol of power. It must be returned in order to keep the balance. It is a gem of great value because it will save many, for it has the power to heal."

"But how will I know where to find them? Where do I find this symbol of power?" Sarah gabbled. "And what balance are we keeping? I just met you. Aren't you assuming a lot? You're very kind, but I don't know what you think you know about me. I'm just a lost little girl."

"You will know them by the birthmark you all share," Ferd continued, almost as if she hadn't spoken at all. "Look at your right hand." He nodded at her encouragingly.

Sara looked at her left hand. In between her thumb and pointer finger, she saw a half moon-shaped birthmark shining a dull red color against her skin.

"I have never seen that before," she said, stunned as she ran her finger over it. *What is going on here? This is getting too strange.* She looked down at her hand again and the mark was still there, a physical reminder that all of this strange stuff was really happening. She stared at him blankly, still hoping to make sense of something that made no sense at all.

"It was hidden," said Ferd. "Another way to keep you safe for a while. We are the Keepers of order in this land. We have been around for many centuries. We maintain the balance between good and evil. For as you know, both always have, and always will be present in this world and others."

"This world and others?" Sara broke in, grimacing at the harsh look they gave her for the interruption.

"Yes, dear. There are seven worlds within one planet, all compressed into dimensions within one space." Maggie recited as if explaining a well-rehearsed fact learned in school, like no I before E except after C.

"I don't think she had that part of the Keepers' education." Ferd explained, as if trying to soften a mild unkindness in Maggie's tone. "But many years ago, for reasons we can't explain yet, evil began to gain a stronghold in the places normally dominated by the forces of good. This evil went by the name of the Garren, a group who has no compassion for others, no kindness, no love, for they were created purely for destruction. They use what they can to corrupt the minds of good people and turn them into unthinking, uncaring slaves who do what they are told. The Garren will use these people to feed and nurture hate in our world. A hate and anger that will thrive eventually destroying everything we value, and our world will end. This is the closest we have come to that point in a long time. And now we have so little time to prepare you. I'm so sorry. You are but one of three souls that have been brought into this world by Iam, the great creator to carry on the work of the Keepers. Olie, our leader, has fought against the Garren for centuries, always keeping them at bay, always ensuring that good is the dominant force. He is not with us now, but you can help with that. You must find the Healing Stone. This object will help to restore the balance. You are one of three children who must find the stone and bring it to Olie."

"All three of you have old and powerful souls," said Maggie. "You will not realize your full potential until you are together again. After creation, your souls were placed into the bodies of children born of his most trusted guardians. Unfortunately, the guardians were destroyed when the Garren rose up and attacked in increasing numbers and with such force that they chose to sacrifice themselves to allow Olie to escape. You three children were quickly gathered and hidden in places we thought the Garren would be least likely to look. We allowed Salius, a trusted Keeper, to choose the places. Apparently, a mistake, since we removed you from a bad situation. We only sensed your distress recently since it had become so strong. That is why we were able to bring you back here. It is our duty to see that you are safe. It was always intended that you would return eventually. And this is the right time, the necessary time."

"We must hurry," Ferd said. "There is much that we need to do, and we cannot be found here with you. We would not willingly lead them to you, but they can sense our presence more easily than yours. I am afraid we have stayed longer than we should."

And as he uttered these words, Ferd and Maggie disappeared in a flash of light.

Chapter Four

In stunned silence, Sara sat alone by the flickering fire, holding the plate full of food that Ferd had given her, the only evidence that she hadn't imagined the whole encounter. She set it down on the log next to her, her appetite suddenly gone. The plate made a sharp clinking sound when it touched the wood- slowly dissolving as if it had never been there.

"Things seem to disappear rather quickly here," she muttered. *Well, out of one bad situation into another*, she thought grimly. Shifting her foot slightly produced a faint rustle, reminding her of the note Ferd had given to her. She reached down, unfolded it, and started to read.

My dear, Sara,

We are so sorry to have to leave you to face this journey alone. Here is what we know of the other two. One is very gifted with music. This is an important ability because, as you know, music soothes even the most savage of beasts. And beasts will be plentiful where you must go. The other has the ability to move things without touching them. Your ability will be revealed to you in time. Both are people of incredible beauty, but be careful, not all beauty is good; evil can hide behind the prettiest things. When you are near enough to the others, you will feel a connection to them and your birthmark will appear; it is how you will know they are the ones you seek. Head straight out on the path. Because of who you are this world is dangerous. Not everyone you meet is eager to help, in fact, to some your death would be preferable to your success. So be careful. Travel in daylight, rest at night, but stay near the path. Do not stray far from it, no matter what you hear. We will help when we can.

With love,

Ferd and Maggie.

Sara sighed and looked down to see that the mark on her hand had disappeared. *This was getting worse. Evil and beasts! People wanting me dead? What have I gotten myself into?* And all this in a letter discussing the danger in an *oh, by the way* manner that made her wonder who she had agreed, or rather been told to help. Don't travel at night. It was night now.

"I'd better stay by the fire and get some rest if I'm to start out to who knows where to find who knows what." Speaking to herself, more out of a need to still her nerves than the expectation that an answer would come floating along the air, Sara looked cautiously about for a comfortable spot to rest by the fire. The eerie silence was broken by a low rumbling that made her jump until she realized it was coming from her stomach, making her wish desperately that she had finished the food before it had vanished. She was still so hungry! Maybe if she slept, she'd forget about it.

Shifting position, her hand connected with the smooth, hard, rim of a plate. The contact made her jump. Looking down, she found the plate perched on the log where she had placed it earlier. The food was fresh, untouched, still looked delicious and the plate appeared to have been filled up again. After a moment's hesitation, in which she decided it must be something Ferd and Maggie had sent in this strange place, she began to devour the food as fast as she could without making herself sick.

When satisfied, Sara stopped and took a deep breath. She felt so full, as if she could easily roll to her destination. This had never happened before. In the future, she would know not to eat quite as much. With a sigh, she placed the plate on the log again. In an instant, it vanished. A trick that was no longer such a surprise.

Now that she had eaten, she was beginning to get very tired. Pushing herself up from the log, she found a smooth, grassy spot and laid out close to the fire. She had just settled down, determined to have a quick nap before heading out to whatever adventure she was supposed to have when she heard a faint rustling in the bushes just beyond the clearing. Heart pounding, she sat up and scanned the darkness for the source of the noise, but saw nothing but trees swaying in the night breeze. Sara waited, senses on full alert, ready to take flight at any second. When no further sound came, she relaxed a little and prepared to stretch out on the grass.

"Must have been an animal," she said aloud, dismissing the incident. "It would really be great if I had a blanket to lie down on," she continued her monologue for the comfort it provided, more than an expectation of a reply.

As she lay slowly back on the ground, her head made contact with a soft, downy object. Surprised, but not unpleasantly so, she sat back up abruptly and found a blue quilt folded neatly where her head had been. *How wonderful. It's like magic! I just seem to think what I need and it is provided somehow.*

"Thank you, whoever you are. I know someone is watching out for me," she whispered and smiled at this discovery.

A soft male voice, so distant she wasn't sure she had heard it, said *You're welcome.* Maggie and Ferd hadn't really left her alone! There was someone else nearby, she could feel it.

"I'm sorry I don't know your name. Okay if I call you Magic Guy?" No answer. "Can you come sit by me? My name's Sara. I'd love to meet you. It would really be nice to have some company. I've never been in the woods before and it's kinda scary."

Again, no answer. All that could be heard was the soft moaning of the wind and rustling of leaves overhead. The fire continued to burn brightly, cracking and popping, providing the small area of shelter with light and heat.

"I'm really a nice person," she continued speaking to the emptiness around her. "If you have time to explain a few things about this place, I'd be so grateful."

Hoping her silent friend was watching, Sara smiled to show her sincerity, patting the ground next to her in invitation to come in from the darkness. Looking around in anticipation of a reply, her hand stopped, mid-pat. Her breath was coming out in icy puffs despite the heat of the fire, and she could no longer hear it crackling. In fact, all sound around her seemed to have ceased; there was a tense stillness now that brought dread with it.

"Magic guy?"

Silence so deep it was almost hollow descended. Her voice was the only thing echoing within the void. The smile froze on her lips when she, once again, heard noises in the form of a rustling in the bushes just beyond the path. Suddenly sending out invitations to unseen things didn't seem like such a good idea.

"Why are you sleeping over there when there's a much more comfortable spot over here?" a thin, reedy voice came from behind the bushes.

All the fine hairs on the back of her neck bristled to attention at the sudden arrival of company she wasn't sure she wanted now.

"Who are you?" Sara clutched the quilt to her chest and tried vainly to see beyond the vegetation to identify the person speaking to her. "Do you know Magic Guy?"

"I am a friend," the voice said. "I can be more helpful than Magic Guy. I can tell you all sorts of things about this world and show you where you need to go. I care for your safety and am terribly concerned about your sleeping out in the open like this. I would hate for you to get sick. Why don't you come over here so I can help you?"

"Why don't you come over here by the fire so that I can see you? The fire is warm and I have a blanket I'd be glad to share. I think it's a lot safer over here. There might be some dangerous creatures out there." Sara remembered the advice that Ferd and Maggie had given her. *Stay on the pathways, stay on the path.*

A slow, humorless laugh rolled through the air in response to her invitation.

"I can assure that I am quite safe. It's you I am worried about. The dark is a much better place to hide. I can't stand that nasty light. Why don't you come over here so that I can help you?"

Each word filled the air with persuasive sweetness carrying with it the promise of not being alone in the dark woods. Sara wondered if the other children Ferd and Maggie mentioned were nearby. *Had they found her already?*

Looking down at her hand for a sign of the half-moon mark she had seen earlier. Sara noted it hadn't reappeared. She had no feeling of instant connection that she'd been told to expect. In fact, the more she thought about it, the whole encounter seemed to have a sudden sense of wrongness. Being alone was a better option than joining her unseen companion.

"No, I don't think so," Sara said. "If you are a friend, tell me who you are. Show yourself."

She kept talking, hoping to prove herself wrong. Maybe it wasn't quite as bad as she was beginning to think. If she could just see the person she was speaking to, she might find she had an ally, someone to travel with. What happened next changed her mind.

"Come here," Soft pleading tone. "Friend, friend, friend, friend," The chanting filled the air.

Sara didn't move, her expression one of caution and a growing fear.

"I am the friend who wants you to come here! Now!" the voice now issued a sharp command.

"No!" Sara shouted back. *I really wish whoever that is would just go away*, she thought desperately. Whoever she was talking to was scaring her now, but she couldn't make them leave.

Immediately after the thought entered her head, she saw a bright flash of light in the area the voice had come from, followed by a loud shriek. The smell of burning hair hung in the air as a dark figure rose from the bushes. At first, it was rather short, like a small child. Then it grew until it reached a height of six foot. Long, skinny arms reached out to her and pale white eyes with no visible pupils shimmered like pearls in its round, smooth face. It had slick white hair over which it wore a dark hooded type of jacket. The thing as she now considered it moved as if it would step out onto the path toward her, but stopped when it got close to the light. Quickly covering its face, it shrank back into the shadows letting out an ear-piercing cry that made Sara wince and cover her ears.

Another flash of light struck the creature. It jerked backwards into the darkness, and fled. She saw the bushes swaying rapidly in a direction that led away from her. Then, there was comforting silence that indicated she was alone. She gulped, trying to draw in air. *What was that hideous thing? It looked like something from a horror movie.* She certainly didn't want to find out what it meant to do with her if it got its hands on her. Tears of relief poured down her face and it took a few minutes to stop her hands from shaking.

She didn't know who or what had intervened to save her, but she had the sick feeling that it would not be so easy to escape another such encounter, if it should happen. And she certainly hoped it didn't.

Shivering and exhausted, she fell to the ground crying and praying to get through this nightmare. Surely this had to be a nightmare, because reality didn't include monsters, food and blankets suddenly appearing out of thin air. But she had someone on her side, or else she would still be engaging in a disturbing conversation with that thing. Maybe the bad part of her dream could be eliminated by the good part. She didn't understand how she wound up here, but if this was indeed a dream, leaving should be as easy as suddenly appearing. Testing her logic, Sara reached out to her invisible savior.

"Hey, Magic Guy. Are you out there? Can you hear me? Please help me out of this. I want to wake up!" she cried, but her pleas were met with total silence.

Feeling more alone than ever, Sara resigned herself to her new reality, wrapped her arms around her legs and curled into a small ball. The warm quilt, which felt real enough, was still underneath her. She sat in what she now considered her one safe spot, rocking back and forth long into the night until she fell into a fitful sleep.

Chapter Five

Sara awoke the next morning refreshed, despite a night that started with unusual dreams. Another reminder that she was indeed awake, reasoning that it was probably impossible to have a dream within a dream. Vaguely remembered images of a shadowy figure standing in the rain flashed through her head. Someone had been trying to speak to her; the words carried an urgent tone, but she couldn't hear what was being said. The occupant of her dream was reaching out, trying to show her something. But whatever it was looked like a blurry blob. She remembered feeling a sense of desperation, like time was running out, not just for her but many others; it was one of those unexplained dream moments in which certainty outweighed actual facts. The figure disappeared, to be replaced by jumbled images of fiery red stones, people running and crying, evil faces grinning in triumph while trees burned and buildings fell around her. Standing amid the chaos, untouched, but affected nonetheless, she heard the soft tinkling of bells. The sound of screams faded, giving way to the roar of waves crashing onto the shore and all became peaceful. Sail boats bobbing on a calm sea, rhythmic slapping of waves on wooden hulls soothed her soul. She was standing on the deck of one of the boats, looking upward, watching crisp white sails snap in a growing breeze. The sound was distinct, making her heart race in anticipation of promised journeys and adventures to be had. This prospect of adventure didn't frighten her as much as offer an escape from the previously tormented visions she'd experienced. The movie in her head transitioned to the cry of seagulls, and finally the soft hissing of water before fading into an uneventful sleep.

Sunlight shining softly through the leaves created a comforting glow that raised her spirits and brought renewed hope that she could get through this. *Maybe I will find the others today. If I'm not alone, I might find my gift and have someone to face the scary things with.* A smile broke out across her face at such a comforting thought. Remembering yesterday's little kindness, she spoke into the air in the hope she might be blessed with another moment like it. She wanted the magic to continue for as long as possible, to convince her she wasn't just being dumped in the middle of a huge mess she was ill-equipped to handle. Because at this time, despite the bright sunny morning and the sound of birds singing in the background, she had doubts about how things were going to work out once she got up and started down the path she had been set upon.

"Hey, Magic Guy, it would be nice to start out with a little breakfast,"

As if on cue, she felt the familiar smooth rim of the plate beside her hand. She looked down to see ripe red strawberries, flaky biscuits, and pale green melons.

"Thank you." She ate with gusto. *I could so get used to eating like this!* she thought. *I could so get used to eating, period.*

"Don't take this for granted", a voice in her head said suddenly. "I will do what I can for you, but promise me you will never get too comfortable with the fact that I always can."

Sara jumped at the intrusion into her thoughts.

"Who are you?" she asked nervously.

"I am Lem," said the voice in her head. "I am the guardian of the forest. I can aid you on this path, but only until you leave the woods."

"Can you tell me where I am going?" Sara asked hopefully.

"All I can tell you is that you must proceed straight down this path until you leave the forest. Beyond that, I cannot say."

"What was that creature in the woods last night?" she asked Lem.

"It was an advance scout of the Garren. He was hoping to lure you off the path so he could take you to them. Do not worry about him now; he is no longer able to bother you, or anyone else for that matter. I do dislike those nasty creatures lurking in my forest. You must move soon, though; the Garren will get suspicious if I do away with too many of them, and they will look in this direction a little more thoroughly." Lem's voice flowed into her head with a soft, soothing tone, but there was an underlying urgency to his words.

Sara finished eating, then walked for several hours, enjoying the warm sunshine on her face and the beautiful trees and flowers she passed on the path. She had not heard Lem for some time now. After he had given her the very little information he had shared earlier, he had stopped speaking entirely. She tried to contact him with her mind like he had, but with no success.

"I guess only you can do that." Still speaking more for her piece of mind than any other reason, she shrugged off the lack of response.

Continuing in silence, Sara tried not to worry. Soon she would reach the end of the path and figure out what to do from there. Letting her mind go blank in the hope that Lem would come through with some answers, she moved on, step after step, down the seemingly endless path, in a warm, relaxing atmosphere filled with only chirping birds and the sighting of an occasional bunny.

"Run!" a thought popped suddenly into her head. "Run, and don't stop until you leave the forest behind!"

37

Sara was startled by the command and the force behind it. She did not hesitate, starting to run as fast as she could. In the woods on either side of her, she could hear gurgling sounds and chilling laughter, could see flashes of light and smell burning hair and flesh. She ran so fast her sides were burning from the effort to catch her breath, but was afraid to stop. She was gasping for air when she saw a brighter patch of sunlight where the forest ended. She sprinted the last few feet out of the forest and stopped just outside the last tree on the path.

"Lem, what happened?" Sara had done what he asked, now she needed an explanation, something to justify her headlong flight through the woods.

Heart racing, she had no idea where to go and why she had just run faster than she had in her entire life.

"They sent the Hateresses to look this time." Lem's answer came softly and from a distance. Even further than before. "The Hateresses are able to travel in daylight; the Garren's scouts are not. This worries me because they must suspect that you are near. You must get away from here as quickly as you can. Find a town and hide among other people. I burned all the Hateresses who dared enter here, but there will be more when they find out what I've done. Leave this area and move quickly down the path. I can no longer help you."

"Wait. What? Don't leave me! What's a Hateress? What am I supposed to do now?" But, even as the words came out of her mouth, her connection to Lem was severed. Where formerly there was at least the feeling of not being completely alone, she now felt a void that made her heart ache. Sara's hands were on her knees as she bent over trying to catch her breath and steady her nerves.

Struggling to gather her thoughts, she slowly straightened and began to walk down the dirt path as quickly as she could, Lem's warnings still fresh in her mind. Afraid to stop, she moved on, glancing fearfully from side to side while crossing the dust covered track winding its way through a broad, flat field. Having no idea where she was, she moved into an unknown world where anything could happen and some very scary things were in pursuit of her.

Chapter Six

The sun was high overhead and the day was becoming warm. There was an occasional rustling in the grass alongside the path, causing the lone traveler to tense up and move faster. Jack rabbits hopped here and there, occasionally one would stop and look at her curiously, its head cocked to the side, deep brown eyes watched her every move. A large bluebird fluttered out of the grass and circled towards the sky. The girl jumped, startled by the sudden movement.

The countryside was beautiful, but other than the animals, there was no sign of a town. Sara had a feeling that she had better find one soon. The sun was sinking lower in the sky. It would be night soon. There were things she didn't want to meet in the dark. Fear made her walk faster, ignoring her aching feet, dry eyes, and mouth. The last time she had anything to drink was the cold water she found with breakfast. She tried several times to visualize food and water, but Lem had meant what he said, and was no longer able to provide her with these things. *That water would be so good right now*, she thought, her mouth felt as if it was filled with sand.

Pressing on, scanning the horizon desperately for any sign of civilization, so anxious to see something, she couldn't quite believe it when she spied the brown A-shaped frame of a roof rising above the hills. At last! Hope of reaching safety soon made her move faster, determined to make it to the house before nightfall.

The further she advanced towards the structure, Sara was pleased to note other rooflines coming into view behind the first. Running now, the buildings below the roofs soon became visible. The first building she saw was a small ramshackle dwelling with flaking blue paint and many weeds growing in the front lawn. Moving cautiously

41

through the yard, and up onto the sagging front porch, tiptoeing carefully across the rotting boards, she knocked timidly on the door. But it was enough for the front door to fall off its hinges and crash onto the floor of the house. Sara jumped back, then leaned forward and peered inside. The house was as empty as its appearance suggested. The small front room was filled with dust, rat droppings, broken boards and little else. There was nothing to indicate that anyone had lived here for quite some time: no furniture, clothing, nothing left of any human presence. Tentatively crossing into the remains of a kitchen, she faced a dirty white sink under a window, with a small metal tower with a long metal handle hanging over it. Sara wouldn't have known what the strange contraption was had she not seen one in an old movie. It was a water pump from a time before modern plumbing. And, just like she'd seen in that movie, she lifted the handle, raising and lowering it a few times to see if any water would emerge. Rusty metal made a grinding noise in protest at being moved after what must have been a long time. The pump jerked beneath her hand, struggling to perform its long-forgotten task. Several attempts yielded nothing except a sore hand, so she gave up and prepared to leave.

Sara had almost reached the front door when she felt a faint rumbling beneath her feet and tingling in every nerve ending in her body. Stomach lurching sickeningly- her blood moved through her body like the tide pulled by the powerful gravity of the moon. Panicking, she picked up the pace to the sound of grinding rocks and the ground shaking as if from a small earthquake. She had just reached the front door when she heard a hissing noise behind her, followed by a dripping sound. Startled, Sara turned in time to see a small amount of rusty water dribbling from the pump in the kitchen.

"That's not possible," she said to herself, as the trickle became steadily stronger, then became a heavy flow of clear fluid.

As Sara watched, amazed, the water flowed from the sink and began to form an airy vapor that floated over her head. She had been too shocked to move as she watched the vapor approach, this new event mobilized her. Just as she turned to run for the door again, the vapor once more turned into water and rained down over her head.

"Oh!" she yelled, shaken by the sudden contact with the ice-cold water. She stood absolutely still, clothing dripping onto the dusty wooden floor, watching as water continued to come from the pump and pour into the sink.

Lem? Sara thought to herself. No answer came. She felt no threat at this sudden strange event, but wondered who or what had come to her aid. Lem had said that he couldn't help her outside of the forest. Driven by the thought of quenching her thirst, she ran to the sink and began to drink the cold water. Cupping her palms to bring it to her mouth, Sara drank greedily, stopping when the icy water gave her the sudden headache that most people called a brain freeze. Tightly closing her eyes while the sudden stabbing sensation slowly subsided, Sara waited out the pain- opened her eyes again- and was amazed to find herself reaching for the water instinctively as if it were part of her. The cool, clear fluid rose and fell with a motion of her fingers- thin rivulets hovering above the sink to fall back with a plop into itself as her hand flattened in a pushing motion. Amazed at the knowledge that she had just discovered her gift- Sara amused herself by flinging the water around for a few minutes- laughing as it obeyed her every command.

"I can control water! That's my power." She spoke the wonderful words to herself before she saw shadows cast by the late afternoon sun across the wet floorboards- a reminder that it would soon be dark. She stepped back onto the rotting porch and looked at the sky again; the sun was getting lower; it would only be a couple of hours now until sunset. She had to move faster to find a safe place to stay the night.

Safety in mind, she quickly searched other houses scattered nearby, only to find they were deserted, too. Urgency to find shelter drove her down the path to see several more houses, but she spent little time at places that were obviously empty. Thankfully, luck was on her side. A short way down the path she came across a few inhabited houses. There were people. At first, she heard them, and then she saw them, two small children and a woman. Excitement made her heart race, as tired legs carried her forward.

"Hello!" she called out, running toward them, almost breathless in her rush to make contact with totally normal people.

Despite her haste, she was smiling brightly at the strangers, who to her surprise, stared at her with shocked looks before running for a nearby house.

"No! Wait. I need your help." Approaching the door they had entered, she knocked loudly. "Please, let me in. I'm all alone. I'm scared. It will be dark soon and there are some bad things out here."

She could hear them moving around inside, but despite her frantic pleas they ignored her.

Puzzled and frustrated, she ran to the next house hoping for a more welcoming reaction. The response was the same. She could see someone inside looking at her suspiciously from behind the curtain, but they would not open their doors when she approached. And it was the same with each of the four houses in this small neighborhood. *What was wrong with these people that they would glare from behind their shutters and not attempt to help a small girl?*

Shocked by this turn of events, Sara paced up and down the grass, aware her every move was being closely scrutinized. Trying not to panic as the sun dipped lower in the horizon, she looked even further down the path for sign of more houses, but she didn't see any. And then, ear shattering screeches and evil laughter sounded from somewhere beyond the houses, from the direction she had just crossed. She needed to hide, and this was not the place to do it. The faces behind the curtains disappeared. They had heard it, too. They were smart enough to be scared but not kind enough to help her.

The sun was almost down now, with no town visible, desperation and fear had her running at full speed back to the first house she had seen, the empty one. Frantically dragging the door back in front of the entrance, she propped it closed with loose boards salvaged from the floor around her. Crawling away from the windows, she hid in a corner, waiting fearfully for any sign of approach by unknown enemies.

They were out there, she had heard them, could still hear them from time to time in the distance. Inhuman screams and incoherent noises cut through the night, followed by long stretches of silence. The ordinary sounds made waiting worse – chirping crickets mingled with the scuffling of wild things moving around in their natural environment – only to give way to the sound of wild, unexpected, unnatural things. And each time they came closer to her abandoned house. Whatever was making them was coming towards her hiding-place. Growling sounds filled the air.

The sky became darker. Footsteps on wood, fingers taping on windows, incoherent whispers, what sounded like sniffing, tentative touch on the rickety door.

Sara tensed, eyes squinting tightly together, willing whatever it was to go away.

Then the sound of thunder and the pitter-patter of raindrops striking the roof. At first softly, then hard and fast like barrels of water being dumped from the sky. A light breeze became wailing winds, buffeting the structure with a force that made the house sway. Shrieks and moans sounded just inches away from her hiding-place, on the other side of the wood wall, before being hustled off, driven away by the storm. And still she waited, afraid to believe she was alone. Water dripped steadily from holes in the roof hitting the floorboards, making indoor puddles while she huddled in her corner, too terrified to move. It seemed like hours before the rain subsided and she fell into a deep exhausted asleep.

Chapter Seven

Next morning, Sara woke up feeling tired and a little disoriented. It took a few minutes to remember last night's events, the eerie sounds of would-be attackers roaming so close to her hiding-place, testing her ramshackle fortifications for an entry point, sniffing around like rabid dogs seeking prey. Heart pounding, she sat upright and studied her surroundings, checking for signs of intruders. But all she saw was the dirty, abandoned room she'd taken shelter in last night. A roach scurried across the floor near her feet and hid in a crack in the wall. Relieved beyond all measure, Sara rushed over to the door.

To get outside, she had to remove boards and slide the broken slab out of her way, but at least it meant she had spent the night undetected. Living to figure things out was a blessing she was grateful for after the crazy day she'd had yesterday.

The sun was already high in the sky. She had slept too long and really needed to get moving soon, but had no idea where to go. Two days in this place and she'd learned that magic exists and so did monsters. Still, she had no idea where she'd landed. But it must be a remote area as she had seen no power lines or telephone poles to indicate technology was present. In fact, all the houses here seemed to be quite basic, with no outside lighting, cement driveways, mail boxes or paved roads. She hadn't seen any roadways other than the path she had walked, certainly not big enough for a car to travel on. Come to think of it, she hadn't seen any cars.

As she studied her surroundings again, she saw the houses she'd been to yesterday, but going back there wasn't an option. She had to find a town. Lem had suggested as much, so obviously towns existed here. People usually settled near towns, didn't they? So, it stood to reason that she would soon find one. Towns were filled with people who might be more willing to help than those she'd seen yesterday.

With a renewed sense of purpose, Sara set out on the path once again, carefully skirting the houses she passed yesterday, which strangely enough seemed to be empty now. There was no movement in or around the dwellings, not even the shifting of a curtain, as she scurried past to the path beyond.

Trying to ignore the emptiness of her stomach and a growing thirst, she walked down the thin dust covered track, past green fields and rows of corn. Mile after mile, she moved on not encountering a single soul, getting more than a little discouraged. She had been walking for quite some time, watching the sun sink lower in the sky, fearful of what she might encounter should she still be on this path at sunset.

Faltering footsteps were steadied by the singing in her head. At first soft, it gained in volume. The unfamiliar tune sung by a female voice she had heard many times before, the same voice that kept her from giving up throughout her difficult childhood was serenading her on her travels. She wanted so badly to talk to that voice but the words wouldn't come, were drowned out by the rising volume of the song. The tune banished all negative thoughts and she began to move faster with a certainty she'd not had before. Speeding up, she began to jog along, mouth moving oddly to the haunting tune in her head. She got so caught up in it, she almost failed to notice that several voices were singing along now. From among the tall stalks of corn on either side of her emerged people dressed in work clothes, carrying bags filled with corn. The group was of varying ages, ranging from the very old to a few children of her age.

They were a cheerful, though weary lot, congratulating each other on a good day's work in the fields and speaking of a day of rest tomorrow. In an oddly well-coordinated move, one of the older people handed her a bag, enabling her to join in with the crowd, the words to the song coming easily to her lips. Mingling freely, she moved towards a large gate behind which she could see the outline of many rooftops. A town! They were headed toward a town. Funny that she hadn't seen it when she was alone, but now it was right there in front of her. The gates were open. Four men who might be guards stood by the entrance with thick clubs in their hands. Their cautious looks gave way to smiles as they saw the approaching group, parting to allow entry into the secured area.

Fearing they might detain a stranger, Sara slunk down behind a tall man making herself as inconspicuous as possible, moving through the gates just as the sun sank into the horizon. Shuffling along in the middle of the group, the small girl took the opportunity to study her surroundings. Buildings of brick and wood with tiled roofs occupied wide stone streets. Neat and well-made, the structures were sturdy but primitive in nature. Once again, affirming her theory that this was not a modern city.

The town was bustling with masses of people hurrying to complete their daily work. People were packing up vegetables and other items that had been sitting on the market stalls, shop doors were closing for the final time that day, and people were calling out goodnight to each other. Knowing the group would soon disperse and go to their respective homes, Sara, having nowhere to stay, had no option but to leave them. She spotted an alley to her right and quickly shuffled down it, disappearing from sight as the group continued on ahead without her.

The alley was long and dark, the only light source a glow cast by the street lamps in the distance. She passed a few closed doors and partially filled trash cans. Finally, she settled herself in a small, closed-off section of the alley behind one of the larger trash can. Sufficiently hidden, her back to the wall, she felt safe enough to study her surroundings. The buildings were all made of brick. There was a door to her right, as well as two doors on the adjoining buildings. The ground beneath her was constructed of smooth dark stones swept free from all debris. Not a single piece of trash littered the ground; in fact, for an alley, it was impressively clean, with not a single rat visible. Not that she wanted to see a rat, it just seemed like they might want to hang out around the trash cans to dine on the goodies inside.

Relaxing in her rodent-free hiding-place, Sara sat quietly trying to gather her thoughts. She had made it to town, but what now? She needed to think before she approached anyone. Her short experience here told her it was a rather primitive place. The stores she'd passed had no electricity; lanterns were everywhere. She'd seen no cell phones, automobiles, or machines of any kind. All the clothing looked like simple cloth material. She couldn't recall seeing jeans being worn by any of the workers she had walked amongst. In the time she had been with the workers on the road, she had only good feelings about them. They were so different from the suspicious, closed off people she had met yesterday. She could only hope that the residents of this town were just the same.

At this point, her stomach started to rumble, and she thought wistfully of the wonderful meals Lem had produced for her in the forest. Knowing she no longer had a magical benefactor, Sara resigned herself to an evening of hunger and loneliness. Only to be startled by the sudden opening of a door to her right. She shrank back in the shadows as a tall boy emerged in the alley with an armful of trash that he stuffed into the wooden barrel next to the door. She saw that he had dark hair and was very handsome, with golden brown skin and dark eyes. His upturned nose was sprinkled with freckles, and lips looked like they might curve up into a smile at any moment. There was an instant flash of recognition that she should know him and he should know her. Sara's breath caught in her throat and her hand itched uncontrollably. But it was too dark to see if the birthmark was visible. She was afraid to move or speak lest she give herself away. She had to be careful, had to be sure who she approached. So, she just sat and watched, afraid to trust in the sudden appearance of what might be one of the people she'd been told she'd meet. It couldn't be that easy.

As if on cue, the boy seemed to sense something also; his head came up suddenly, and he looked directly at her as she hid in the shadows.

"Who's there?" he called softly.

"What's the matter, son?" she heard a voice directly behind the boy say.

A tall, redheaded man appeared and placed a hand gently on his shoulder.

"Oh, it's nothing, Father. Just thought I heard something in the alley," He had a look of confusion on his face, like he felt like she did but was scared by the sudden revelation. She saw him look down at his hand for a second, rubbing at the space between his left thumb and pointer finger, blinking and rubbing the area again. The boy took a step or two towards her but was stopped by his father's strong arm.

"It's probably Burley's cat," the older man said, gently guiding the boy back inside. But his calm tone belied the worried look he cast toward the dark alley.

Though every instinct wanted to reach out to the boy, Sara did not budge from her hiding-place. Fear kept her firmly planted in her safe spot, trying to blend in with the stones behind her. Remaining here meant she was alive and would continue to be alive until she was sure the boy was someone she could trust.

Alone once again, she continued to stare at the doorway, hoping that somehow this boy she thought she knew would come back and make everything clear.

Chapter Eight

It was still dark when Sara woke, slipping out of her hiding-place to walk to town. Staying in the shadows, she looked fearfully about her, on high alert for signs of the guards she had seen at the gates. But there was no movement from that direction or any other nearby. As far as she could see, she was alone, and undetected. The town was asleep and shuttered in for the night, so she took the opportunity to survey her surroundings. Staying as close to the buildings as she could, using the darkness as a cloak, she crept timidly past shop windows, the goods within illuminated by dim street lamps. Rows of sweets on a flat display table teased her, so close yet so unattainable.

In the next store, painted images of bread loaves and cakes beckoned her from just beyond the locked door. *Matther's Meats*, *Miss Whatley's Sweet Breads*, *Freeman's Candy Shop*. One by one, she passed the boldly titled windows, fingerprints smearing the glass with the desire to burn through and eat the contents within. Caught up in her hunger, she forgot for a moment that she was supposed to be invisible, walking further from the shelter of the building than was wise. But she was quickly reminded of the danger of being discovered by a sudden movement to her right. Startled, she ducked into the dark opening of a nearby alley. Observing the streets from the safety of darkness, she soon saw the source of the noise was a small black cat running across the narrow street. In an eerie moment of silent communication, the animal stopped suddenly and turned to look at her with odd glowing green eyes. Staring back in fascination, she got the sensation of a command to follow. Unable to resist, she crawled hesitantly toward the cat, which, seeing it had her attention, turned and walked towards a raised stone structure in the middle of a wide courtyard.

Having led her there, the furry body skirted around the structure from which a faint gurgling sound could be heard and disappeared from sight. Drawn by the familiar sound of moving water, Sara continued forward, and was soon rewarded with the tantalizing sight of a fountain circulating silvery fluid. Unlike the food she saw earlier, she could reach the water. Kneeling at the fountain wall, she cupped her hands together and drank greedily. Staying as low as she could to avoid being seen, she took in as much water as she could, stopping only when she began to feel a bit sick. Once satisfied, she sat back against the fountain and tried to come up with a plan of action. She'd watch the boy a little longer, and see if the birthmark reacted again. She had to know if what she'd felt when she saw him was real or just wishful thinking on her part. Having been a helpless victim for the first part of her life, she was not willing to place herself in that position again. If she were to entrust her life to someone, she had to be certain they were all she expected them to be.

Feeling hopeful now that she had a plan, Sara enjoyed the soothing sound of the water, sitting there until she heard the faint stirring of movement from some of the nearby buildings. Not wanting to be discovered just yet Sara decided to return to her hiding-place. Staying low, with the last of the night providing cover, she moved back toward the alley where she'd first seen the boy. As she crawled to her hiding-place, Sara was surprised to see it already occupied. The boy was sitting there waiting for her with a thick slice of bread. This encounter did not scare as much as delight her. The familiar feeling of it was like coming home.

"Hello Sara," He scooted sideways, patting the ground next to him and offering her the piece of bread. "I had a feeling you'd be hungry."

Smiling brightly as she sat next to him, Sara accepted the food from a boy who she intuitively knew hated Brussels sprouts, loved to ride his pony named Jewel, was good at carving wood and playing his flute, and was now as close to her as if they'd grown up in the same house. A million thoughts and memories flooded her head. And all they had to do was sit there not saying a word, becoming acquainted by some kind of magical bond. When she did talk, it wasn't because she had to, but felt she needed to express appreciation for his kindness. His name rolled off her lips easily as it she'd said it many times before.

"Thank you, James." Her hand burned slightly. She glanced down at the birthmark and could see the half-moon shape appear on her hand, illuminated by the dim light of a candle he placed next to him.

Though they'd only just met, they began to talk like old friends who'd not seen each other for a long time. He knew she'd just learned that she could do something weird with water, and she knew he could use music to make wonderful things happen. These gifts which made them different enough from others to be special souls were also the gifts that brought them closer together.

This strange reunion continued for several hours until people stirring in their houses could be heard all around them. James snuffed out the candle, not willing to reveal their hiding-place. Silently shushing her with a finger to his lips, he sought to keep their location secret. Crouching low, her new best friend peeked around the trash cans to see if anyone was there. She knew he wanted to keep her safe and was trying to find a way to get her out of the alley without attracting attention. James tensed up as a door opened to their left. He glanced around the trash can, moved away from her for a few agonizing seconds, before turning back, grabbing her hand and pulling her into the alley. As faint golden rays of sunshine spread into the entrance, James faced the red-haired man she had seen with him earlier. "James, what are you doing up so early? I got worried when I noticed you weren't with the others…"

The man stopped talking and looked expectantly at Sara. "Hello?"

"Father, this is Sara," James began, but was unable to continue with an inventive explanation for her presence at his side. "She's lost. She needs our help." Was all he could say without lying.

Of all the things she had learned about James so far, in their odd kind of instant knowing, she knew he couldn't lie to his father. An intense look was shared by the two males in which something significant passed.

For just an instant, Sara saw moisture build up in his father's eyes. Then, just as quickly, the moment passed and the man turned to the girl with a sad, almost resigned expression she didn't understand.

"Hello, Sara. My name is Mr. Marsden." It looked for a moment that he might say something else, but noises from the street made him look nervously over his shoulder and usher both children towards the door. "We will certainly help you, but first, let's go inside. Are you hungry?" This last part he said as he made sure Sara and James were safely in front of him and well on their way through the door. The man moved back to allow them to enter as he looked thoughtfully at her. She knew he had family but was a little overwhelmed when she walked into a household full of people. There were at least seven others in the room, six of them children ranging in ages from three to sixteen. The children were introduced from youngest to oldest, starting with Bella, who was three, Thurston four, Abbey seven, Charles eight, Daniel twelve, and Harry was thirteen. There was also a small blonde woman who Mr. Marsden introduced as his wife Ella. James was fourteen years old and couldn't be more different in appearance to this family; his light brown skin in stark contrast to the rosy cheeks of the Marsdens. He was just as tall as his younger brothers; that was all he had in common with them. But, despite the obvious differences, he seemed to share a deep bond with this family. They treated him well. Love definitely dwelt in this house; Sara could feel it all around her. She soaked up the family warmth while introductions were made.

The Marsdens were a very friendly lot; always smiling and joking amongst themselves. All-in-all, this was a wonderful experience for Sara, but what struck her as strange was that they didn't ask her a lot of questions, though they'd expressed concern about how tired and hungry she looked. They appeared to have just sat down at a table covered with all sorts of delicious foods. Sara was ushered into a chair, and her plate piled high with food. She was seated next to James, and as she quickly looked down at his right hand; she noticed the birthmark was clearly visible. He seemed surprised to see it and she showed him the matching one on her hand. When she tried to say something to him about it, she was gently shushed by Mr. Marsden and encouraged to eat breakfast.

It was not until the meal was finished and the other children given the task of clearing the table and taking the dishes to the kitchen with Mrs. Marsden that James father began to speak. He had asked Sara and James to remain with him, pointing at last to the marks on their hands.

"It seems the time has come," he said, as he watched the two children examining the marks. "I was told to expect something great to happen with you, James. I told you that you were a gift to us, and I have enjoyed the privilege of being your father. Now, one of your own has come to help you fulfill your destiny." Taking a deep breath, the older man continued his strange narrative. "James, I have always told you that you were not our natural son, that you were placed with us by a man who told us it was important that your location be kept secret. He said that he could not tell us where you came from and why he was hiding you, that it was best for us not to know too much, for this could bring great danger. We took the responsibility of caring for you very seriously and love you just as much as our natural born children. But, now that Sara is here, the few things that he told me are very clear. He said that another one like you would arrive suddenly, and that it would be necessary for you to leave and complete a mission for the good of us all. Your reaction to each other, the matching marks on your hands tells me that she must be the one he spoke of. We will have to prepare for your departure soon. I fear that it will not be long before you must go."

"No, Father, I cannot leave you all behind. We will all go," James said with a determined expression.

"We will discuss this later, son. Sara looks exhausted. Let's find her a place to sleep."

Sara was given a soft bed in the girls' room, where she soon fell asleep.

The next few weeks were wonderful. Sara and James talked incessantly. He shared images and experiences of growing up with his brothers and sisters, and she shared her own of growing up with the Finklesteins. She tried to dwell on the things she enjoyed like school and the books she'd read, but James was able to see the loneliness and sorrow she had felt all those years.

"I'm so glad that you were placed with this family," she told him. "That Salius guy made a good choice for you."

"But he didn't for you," James said sadly.

During her stay, James shared his incredible gift of music. He had a lovely flute carved from mahogany and played with such skill that everyone stopped what they were doing and stood entranced at the sound. James often played for a short time every evening to help calm the other children to sleep. His music had the strangest effect on the household, the calming notes bought out a feeling of rightness about the world, a deep peace that soothed the listener into the deepest sleep. Though it was lovely to listen to, it didn't have the same hypnotic effect on Sara. She could enjoy it but wasn't as entranced as the others. She was guessing it had something to do with their unique bond that went deeper even than the love he had for his family. Sara had never known family life like this, there was so much love here. This was just like the family that she had always wanted. They worked hard, but did it joyfully, with everyone helping to do the chores. Hard work was something that Sara was used to, but she was not used to having anyone help her, or even care if she needed it. It was wonderful to have someone to work side by side with like this.

As hard as they worked, they played just as hard. And play was something that Sara had never been allowed to do. While with the Marsden's, she learned to play tag, leap-frog, and hide-and-seek, games most children had already learned before the age of twelve. The other children seemed to sense that she was new at this and they did their best to educate her on all the basics. She was really getting good at playing. She had mastered the game they called stickball. It was kind of like baseball except they used sticks and a ball fashioned out of a hollow gourd covered with fabric. She had an incredibly strong swing and could hit the ball far out into the field.

Her team won most of the games they played and she soon became accustomed to enjoying herself.

Thoughts of her good fortune were going through her head as she and James helped the others tidy up before dinner one night. The strong bond they shared enabled him to pick her thoughts up effortlessly.

"Maybe, when we have done what we are supposed to do, you can come to live with us permanently," said James, with a big smile on big face, as if they would soon embark upon a short adventure. "My family is so wonderful. I know that they would love for you to stay with us forever."

"That would be wonderful," said Sara, trying not to voice the doubt she was beginning to feel more strongly as time went on.

"Yes, it would!" piped in James's two younger sisters, breaking Sara's train of thought. They then pummeled James and Sara with pillows they had dragged in from the bedroom.

"Just what we need, another sister; ewww!" his brothers shouted as they jumped up and joined in the pillow fight. As they did every night, the children laughed and played for a while before settling down to help Mrs. Marsden prepare dinner. Sara was used to their routine, welcoming the normalcy, aware that she was a sort of guarded secret to the outside world. In town, she was not introduced to the neighbors. In fact, her presence was carefully hidden from the people around her. She saw both James' parents often look at her with concern and a strange kind of sadness. Mr. Marsden was a carpenter who worked for several businesses in town. When he came home in the evening, he would have news about the people there. Each day he arrived more disturbed about the things he saw. He had been hearing reports of increasingly hostile behavior exhibited by the people dwelling outside the village. At first, there were little arguments about petty things, arguments that were easily resolved by the clearer-headed townsfolk. Compromises were made and peace was kept. But, according to Mr. Marsden, there were some farmers who had come very close to violence; threats were made and punches almost exchanged.

James's father was concerned about the children going too far from the house. They were forbidden to play outside the town gates, and he told them they were no longer to play with the farmer's children who sometimes came into town with their parents.

"I don't know who to trust anymore," he said. "It's sad because we have known some of these people for years, and now I don't feel like I know them at all. Farmer Polk came into town the other day and looked at me so coldly. I asked him what I had done to make him angry, and he just shrugged and said he didn't know what I meant. Then he asked how the family was doing and if there were any new additions that I might want to tell him about. I really didn't like the way he was scrutinizing me as he waited for an answer, so I just told him no. But I could tell he didn't believe me." A pause followed before he added, "Something bad is coming."

It wasn't long before he was proved right.

One evening, he arrived home looking very worried. "There is something terrible happening," he said. "The farmers who come into town to sell their produce have gone too far, they have doubled the prices for their goods and are offering only the worst of their crops. Farmer Cable and his boys just got into a fist fight with Frank Pauls and some of the other merchants who objected to what they were doing. They were forced to run for their lives and lock the gates. I don't understand; this has never happened before.

Some of the farmers have begun to ask about a blonde girl who came into town several days ago. They want to know where she went and are offering a lot of money to learn where she is. You are not safe here. I'm afraid it's time for the two of you to leave." He looked at James and Sara with tears in his eyes.

As he spoke again, he was busily packing a bag with fruit and bread. "James, you must take your brothers and sisters to your Uncle Tim's house. I cannot bear the thought of this evil affecting any of my children. Your mother and I will stay and act as if everything is normal. This will give you all a chance to escape."

James, his face stricken, grabbed his father's hand tightly. "No, Father. We will all go together!"

Mr. Marsden pushed James roughly away from him. "You will do as I say, young man!" And, turning his back on James, he called the other children to him. With only a short explanation, the children were all led to a trap door located in the kitchen floor and ushered down the steps into a passageway.

"You know what you have to do now," he said, looking sternly at James once more.

"Father, please!" he sobbed as he grabbed at his hand again.

The tall man looked down at him, his face beet-red, as if he were trying hard not to break down and cry.

"Son, I have lived long enough to see many things happen in this land. I know of evil that threatens our existence every day. We all know it's out there, but are afraid to believe that it will come to our doors. Now it is here, and I will not let it take you or the other children. I believe that you are someone who can make a difference, now please do as I say and go!"

James cast one last agonized look at his parents. His mother choked back tears as she fiercely hugged the children and ran back up the steps to the kitchen. Without looking back, James's father mounted the steps and closed the trap door, leaving the children in total darkness.

Chapter Nine

The children stood in stunned silence for a few minutes, listening to the parent's footsteps overhead as they walked away with a finality that made their hearts sink. The silence was finally broken by the crying of the three youngest children. Sara pulled them close to her while James took a lantern down from the wall and lit it. She could tell he was scared, but being the oldest, and possibly one of the reasons they had to leave home in the first place, he steeled himself to be the grown up for his siblings. When she tried to speak to him about this, he shook his head and turned away. "There's a tunnel entrance over there," he said flatly, walking to the opposite wall, pulling aside a standing shelf to reveal an opening in the wall.

After a short inspection, he stepped through and Sara gently guided the others after him. When all the children were inside, she stepped through and pulled the lightweight shelf across the hole again. They were now in a narrow, musty tunnel lined with stones. In the dim light of the lantern, Sara could only see a few feet ahead of her, but it looked like the tunnel had been dug some time ago; the dirt beneath their feet was packed solid, and there was moss growing on the stones.

"My father said this tunnel was dug by smugglers a long time ago," said James. "He found it when he was a boy and told me about it a few years ago, said it was our secret, a way out in case of emergency. Almost like he knew." His words were short and choked with emotion. "Stay close to me."

Turning to walk down the tunnel, the light held high in his shaking hand, James led the group away from home and toward an uncertain future.

They walked for a long time, stopping for a few short breaks to allow the smaller children to rest and sip water out of the pouches they had been given. They proceeded without speaking much. None of them had any idea exactly why they were in this dark and scary place but trusting their older brother to lead them to safety. Sara, concerned for the children's well-being, urged them to continue walking, offering words of encouragement as they proceeded, step by step down the narrow tunnel. James was silent; his back stiff as he steadfastly led them into the unknown.

After what seemed like forever, James stopped suddenly, and raised a hand to halt their progress. Sara moved up to stand right behind him. She could feel cool air flowing in from the end of the tunnel and see the faint glow of moonlight on the dirt floor.

"Uncle Tim's house is not far," James said. "If we walk a little longer, we should be there soon."

As he neared the entrance, Sara grabbed his arm.

"Wait," she said in a hushed voice. "I've been told that it's best not to travel by night. It's probably not a whole lot better during the day, either, but I'd say night is still worse."

Not wanting to alarm the children further, Sara shared memories of the things she'd encountered weeks ago with James.

"Let's just spend the night here in the tunnel."

James looked for a moment as if he might argue with her, but then nodded.

They moved back from the entrance and helped the children to lie down. Sara and James talked to them soothingly and quietly. Normally James would have pulled out his flute and played one of his hypnotic tunes, but being afraid to draw attention to themselves, he kept quiet.

Luckily, the stress and extra activity had tired the young ones and they fell asleep quickly. Sara sat down beside James and gently took his trembling hand. Comforted by the contact, he composed himself and gripped her hand tightly.

"We'll have to leave them with your uncle tomorrow and go on alone," she said.

"I know," he answered. "Will I ever see any of them again?"

"I don't know. I wish I could tell you that everything will be ok. All I do know is that we are supposed to do something to make this situation better. Something about locating someone just like us and finding the Healing Stone that will somehow make this all better. I'm sorry that I can't tell you more. I don't know anything else. I just don't understand this yet, and I'm not quite sure how this will turn out. Frankly, I'm scared to death about what's ahead of us, but I'm more afraid of what will happen if we don't do anything."

Sara and James stayed holding hands for quite some time, trying to give each other comfort in a world gone mad. Nothing made sense and they felt numb and completely overwhelmed by the events of the day. They sat together in the quiet night, contemplating a bleak future, until exhausted they fell into a deep sleep punctuated occasionally by shared visions of red stones and dark scary things staring at them from the darkness with bright yellow eyes.

Chapter Ten

Early the next morning, awakened by the first rays of sunshine, James and Sara rose and began to wake the children. Stretching, yawning and being as quiet as possible, they ate some fruit and prepared for the last part of their journey to Uncle Tim's house.

The group ventured outside the tunnel and silently started down the path. They had only been walking for a short time when they heard shouts from the direction of the town, as if a great fight was taking place. Other loud noises followed and smoke filled the air. Panicked, the children picked up their pace until they were running down the road, thinking only of reaching safety. They didn't slow down until the town was well behind them. Huffing and puffing, the group continued their journey until James pointed to a large tree to the left of the path. The children's faces lit up as they realized. Uncle Tim's home was nearby. Now hopeful, they rushed to the base of the tree with renewed energy and pulled at the thick rope suspended from its branches. A long metal tube descended, turning to scan the crowd before disappearing back into the leafy treetop. A short time later, a platform appeared, and the children stepped onto it and were pulled upward.

They were greeted at the top by a tall man with fiery red hair who closely resembled James's Dad. *This must be Uncle Tim*. He hugged each of the children tightly and ushered them into his house, which was built atop the branches of this unusually large tree. The structure was impressive, two stories high with windows on every side, providing Uncle Tim with an uninterrupted view of the land below. A wide porch with railings and posts carved in the shape of animals surrounded the house.

Plants graced the outside of the deck, with vines trailing all along the walls of the home, blending with the tree's leaves to effectively camouflage the dwelling from being spotted below. Sara was sure she would have never found this place if the children hadn't known it was here.

The inside of the house was just as impressive as the outside. Built in the center of the trunk, Sara found herself staring in amazement at the thick beams of the ceiling and smooth floors glowing from frequent polishing. There were several large pieces of furniture arranged artfully throughout the first floor and all this located almost at the very top of a tree tall enough to view the town miles away from them. Everything was lovely and well-kept for a bachelor's home. James had said there was no Mrs. Uncle Tim and no cousins to keep him company. He basically lived for and adored James's father and his family.

The man stood uncomfortably close to Sara, watching her curiously as introductions were made. She could tell he was suspicious of her arrival at this time of turmoil, but was reserving judgement in order to not frighten his nieces and nephews.

"This is Sara," James introduced her, grabbing her hand for moral support. "She was staying with us when some bad people came into town."

"I've seen what's happening in town." he said, pointing to the scene visible from his windows. "Your father came to me last week and told me that if anything bad should happen, I should not go into town. He wanted me here to look after his children. It was almost as if he knew."

Smoke rose from several fires burning in the distance while Uncle Tim watched silently. After James explained their situation, Uncle Tim said, "I'm glad that your father was able to get you out in time. What happened to your parents?" His voice was husky with worry as he continued to stare at Sara with a strange expression.

"We had to leave without them. Father insisted on it," James replied.

Having listened passively for a few minutes, Daniel and Harry approached, with a grim look on their faces. They had not said much up to this point, having followed their father's instructions to do what James said, as he was the oldest. But now that they'd had time to think, they regretted not asking questions, not insisting James go back for their parents.

"Now that the girls are safe, we men should go get Mom and Dad!" they cried, as they puffed out their chests and tried to appear confident and tough.

"You most certainly will not!" Uncle Tim replied, shooing the boys back to the other side of the room with the others. "If anyone is to go into that craziness, it will be me. James, you can stay and watch after the children. I'll go into town, get Bob and Ella and bring them back here."

There were groans of protest from Daniel and Harry as he said this but they did as they were told, moving back to join their sisters and stare at him sullenly from across the room.

"No, Uncle Tim, you can't do that," James said, looking directly at him.

"And why would that be?" his uncle asked him grimly.

"Because we can't stay, and the children have to be kept safe. I promised Father. The situation is too bad in town now. There's no guarantee that you'll make it back here. You have to stay and we have to go on without them."

Lowering his voice, so that the children could not hear him, James whispered, "I am counting on you to keep them safe," as he continued to watch his uncle closely.

"What makes you think that I would ever allow the two of you to leave here while all that craziness is going on out there?" Uncle Tim looked at him incredulously.

"Because I think we are the reason that it's happening." Sara said, pointing towards the fires. "I think whoever did that is looking for me. And because I have some kind of connection to James, they are after him, too."

Tim gave her a puzzled look. It took a while, but James and Sara explained the events that had brought her to this land. They talked softly to keep the other children from hearing them. Tim was a skeptical at first, but when she told him about Ferd and Maggie, the disbelief on his face slowly turned to shock.

"I know those names; they're Keepers. We are aware of them, but we don't see them much. They appear every so often and seem to like knowing how things are going with us. I have talked to them once or twice over the years. They are very old and wise. Your Father knows them a little better than me."

"Then you believe us; and you will help us? You will let us leave." James asked, looking directly into his uncle's eyes. Sara got the feeling that James was doing something besides talking. As he stared at his uncle, he seemed not to be able to look away. She felt a hum in the air. Some kind of energy was building. Uncle Tim's eyes began to glaze over and he looked back at James as if everything he said made perfect sense. Sara noticed that James also seemed to be doing something to affect the children as well, for they suddenly went very quiet, simply staring back at him with vacant eyes.

Uncle Tim nodded solemnly and turned to the other children.

"Well, little ones," he said cheerfully, "let's get you all cleaned up and get a decent meal in your bellies." As he spoke, he led them towards the back of the house. The kids followed him quietly and unquestioningly, not even seeming to notice that James and Sara were not coming too. "What did you do?" Sara asked as the others filed into the other room like docile lambs.

"The only thing I could do," James answered. "I controlled their minds and made them do what I needed them to do."

"But what about your Mom and Dad? Sara asked, puzzled. "Couldn't you have done that to them, too, made them come with us?"

"It never worked on my parents. I don't usually do this if I don't have to, but my family can't be placed in danger. Now, let's get out of here quick!"

James turned stiffly and Sara followed- both boarded the platform, lowering it to the ground before walking away without looking back once.

Chapter Eleven

"How long have you been able to do the mind control thing?" Sara asked James.

"Not long, maybe a year. I'm not very good at it most of the time. I told my dad about it, and he said that I better not be using that against anyone. I admit I did try it on him once when I got in trouble, but it didn't help. I only got in trouble worse. That's when he made me promise that I would not use it on people again. I hope he understands that I had to do it this time. I couldn't let Uncle Tim go back into town, and I know he wouldn't have said yes to us going off by ourselves. I sure couldn't let Daniel and Harry go and do something stupid."

Sara nodded at this, and they picked up their pace a bit as they continued down the road.

"But how do you do it?" Sara asked after a moment's silence.

"I don't know. I concentrate, and sometimes it happens the way I want it to," he answered in a clipped voice.

"But –"

"Look, Sara, I don't know a lot about this yet," he snapped. "And I really don't want to talk about it right now. I just want to get away from here before I change my mind about doing this, ok?"

Sara looked at him and nodded, closing her mouth quickly to hide her shock.

"Sorry," he added before turning back to the road.

As it had still been early when James and Sara headed off again, they were able to travel for several hours, stopping only once to eat. There wasn't much food left since they hadn't restocked at Uncle Tim's, so they ate sparingly.

"Where do you think we will meet our last companion?" asked James anxiously.

"I don't know," said Sara. "We'll have to wander aimlessly until something happens. That's what I did before I met you."

"Well, I guess it worked, but it would be nice to have some sort of plan."

Sara nodded absently, and they continued to walk.

They encountered few people along the way. In fact, they made great efforts to avoid contact with everyone. Senses on high alert, the pair watched for any movement in their vicinity, quickly hiding behind trees to avoid being seen. This hide-and-seek method was working well for most of the day, until one time they ducked behind a large tree and were greeted by a tall woman with long, scraggly, gray hair.

"What are you doing?" she asked, causing both children to jump and squeal in surprised shock. "Are you playing a game?"

Sara stepped closer to James and both backed away towards the path. The woman slowly followed, her eyes never leaving Sara's face as she talked.

"I have been watching you two for some time now, and I have to say you are very odd children. Are you lost?"

"No, we are simply on our way to town," James said with a slight tremor in his voice.

"What town might that be?" the woman asked casually, watching every move they made.

"The town where our very large and overprotective family lives," said Sara, gripping James's arm.

"Yes, and I'm sure they will miss us if we are not there very soon," James piped in, stepping backwards at a faster pace. "Well, you'd better hurry then," the woman said, smiling slightly.

"The town is still several miles off. and the sun will be going down in a couple of hours. It won't be safe for two children out here in the dark. One can never tell what might happen."

The woman stayed on the path, watching them intently as they turned and ran away as fast as they could. They did not slow down until they rounded a bend, and the woman was no longer in sight.

"Do you think we lost her?" Sara asked as she looked back toward the dirt path.

"I think so," panted James, trying to catch his breath. "She was right, you know. We do need to find a place to stay. It will be dark soon and it's not safe for us out here."

Sara's steps slowed as they proceeded down a road which closely resembled a road they had already passed three times, with the same fenceposts and bunches of bluebells. She would have put it down to local customs, decorating all the posts, but James found it strange that the post had the exact same markings on it; that it was far too much of a coincidence. It had to be the same post, but how and why was this happening?

"But there's nothing out here." James said, looking dismally down at the little dirt devils forming on the path around them. "I don't like the feeling in the air. We need to hide. And I mean soon."

Sara understood the urgency in his voice – she felt what he was feeling. Anticipation of danger made her skin itch, just like she knew his was. On the surface, anyone watching, would see that they were walking along an ordinary road. But to them something about this particular road was becoming creepier by the second.

"You grew up here. Is it supposed to take this long to get to the next town?"

A slightly confused pause followed and James shook his head. "No. We should have reached Rees by now. This is not right."

Both children stopped dead in their tracks. Whereas just a moment ago the sky had been pink and gold, the colors cast by the setting sun, it now had a sickly green tint to it. Sara heard a faint popping sound, and both she and James began to walk towards a concentrated area of thicker green that had appeared directly in front of them. Unable to resist their intense curiosity, they walked towards the light that had begun to resemble a bright doorway. Perhaps they had wandered too close without being aware. The next thing Sara and James knew, they were surrounded by a light so intense they couldn't see a thing, and the next, they were back on a path again.

For an instant, the pair was too stunned to move, but after a slight breeze blew away the last of the green mist, found they were still facing the possibility of being caught, wherever they were, outside when the sun went down. Of all the things that suddenly weren't clear, the one thing that was, was that they weren't in the same place anymore. The fields were green and the sky was blue but the fence posts were gone and the path paved with tiny polished stones now ran through rolling hills, and there was a faint trail of smoke in the distance. The smoke wafted upward in a thin trail that indicated it came from a chimney rather than an open fire – and that meant a house. Sara and James stared at the smoke and shared one thought. *Safety.* Aware, that being caught out here in the darkness was not an option they cared to explore, they moved eagerly toward safety.

Chapter Twelve

Sara and James followed the smoke, which for some reason seemed further away with each step they took. The sky was growing dark and the faint howling from some kind of animal could be heard in the distance. Following that was something worse, an unearthly giggling that made the hair stand up on the back of their necks.

"I think we can both agree that we need to get off this road," James was the first to speak, or rather whisper in the growing darkness.

"I don't know if leaving the road is such a good idea." Sara looked about her worriedly.

"You remember what Ferd and Maggie told me," James gripped her arm and spoke softly, trying not to attract the attention of the scary things they knew must be out there. "But that was there and I'm sure we are now somewhere else completely, so let's find a place to hide."

Nodding at the weird way that made sense, Sara allowed James to lead her away from the pebbled road and towards the only thing resembling shelter – a partially destroyed rock building located just a few feet from the road. It was hardly what one might call a decent hiding-place, but it was basically the only hiding-place nearby.

With three and a half walls and half a roof, the structure was hardly impregnable but would have to do. Scrambling through the fallen rocks, they sat with their backs pressed to one of the intact walls, ready to confront whatever horrors might come charging at them. Though certain they were meant to do something special they weren't quite sure what it was, only that they should live long enough to do it. James reached in the bag they had brought with them, and grabbed an apple, the last of the food his father had given them. He handed it to Sara who took a bite and then returned it to him. Back and forth, they passed the fruit, enjoying what might be their last bit of food for a long time, not sleeping a wink as they listened to spooky noises that, thankfully, did not come close to the ramshackle building.

"I miss my family," James whispered.

"I miss your family, too," Sara admitted with a sad smile.

"We'll do whatever they need us to and get back to them. Once we do you'll never have to leave." James promised, hugging her tightly.

A howling in the distance. They stopped talking once again, and stayed huddled together for comfort. Fear kept them alert as the cloak of night was peeled back to reveal the pink-golden sheen of a new day. It was not until the sun revealed more of the land around them that the exhausted pair felt secure enough to take a short nap.

The sun was still high in the sky when they woke again, feeling as if they'd been roused by an internal alarm clock. The urgent sensation of having to get up and move on was overwhelming and not to be ignored. Bleary-eyed, Sara and James hobbled out of their makeshift shelter and proceeded down the road to some place they just knew they had to be. Open fields gave way to groves of trees, the path wound on between them making what lay ahead harder to see. Small openings that might have been paths could be seen from time to time.

Having no actual idea of where they were going, the travelers soldiered on until instinct took over and showed them the way. James seemed to find it easier going than Sara, moving towards a part of the road that branched out beyond some shrubs and was not easily seen from there. He followed this new part of the trail for a short time before stopping to speak.

"Look over there, Sara," he said, pointing to the left of the road as if he weren't at all surprised to see what was there. Set slightly away from the path was a small house. It looked well-kept, with a trimmed lawn and several well-tended rose bushes lining the path to the house. To the side was a small vegetable garden, and they could see a young man tending to the plants. His thick, dark hair was pulled back and tied with a leather strap. His olive skin bore a fine sheen of sweat as he pulled heads of lettuce from the dirt and placed them in a cart next to him. Hearing the sound of footsteps on gravel, the hard-working boy looked up as they approached. The crescent shaped marks on James and Sara's hands itched so much they looked down to see them dark and clearly visible. Their reaction mirrored the boy's own surprised expression, staring at his left hand before greeting them with a smile of instant recognition. They too felt drawn to him and picked up their pace to reach him. As they got closer, however, the look on the boy's face changed. It was now one of fear.

"What's wrong?" James and Sara said together, as he tried to wave them away from him.

"Yes, what's wrong, Thomas?" said a deep voice.

Sara and James turned to find a very handsome man standing directly behind them. His wavy, dark hair the same color as the boy's, his eyes were a deep brown. He was dressed neatly in a dark pair of trousers and coat, looking very much, a man of leisure compared to the Thomas he was addressing. The man smiled, dazzling them with the brilliance of his white teeth.

"Well, well, who would you two be?" he said, patting Sara on the head with a soft hand. "It's not possible that these two lovely children have scared you, is it, Thomas? No, I'm sure they didn't. Perhaps you're just tired. You've been working out in the sun all day. We both have. Why don't we all go inside and get some dinner. They do look a bit worn from traveling for days."

Sara saw James frown a little at that statement. The man seemed to know a lot for a stranger.

"There's dust on your clothes, you look so tired and I don't recognize you from around here," the explanation rolled off the man's lips easily while watching James closely.

James nodded, cautiously satisfied for the moment. After all, this man looked so nice and he wanted to believe they were finally safe. The mark on their hands proved that this was the young man they were looking for and this had to be his family so they would be alright. Sara looked at Thomas once more; the look of fear was gone from his eyes now, replaced by a look of uncertainty.

Slowly, he followed them into the house which was just as neat inside as out. Simple wood floors were covered in home-made rag rugs. A table sat next to a fireplace, and there was a cozy seating area in the other half of the room. A fire crackled merrily in the fireplace, and Sara could smell something delicious cooking in a pot there. The nice man settled them at the table and gave Thomas instructions to give Sara and James some of the stew cooking over the fire. Thomas carried two bowls to the pot and spooned a little of the stew into each. He began to speak to Sara and James as he did so, deliberately slowing his movements.

"Who are you and how do you happen to be all the way out here by yourselves?" he asked, still dribbling stew into the bowls with his work roughened hands. Sara found the questions rather strange because she was sure he knew their names and a lot more. The birthmark they shared was flaring brightly on their hands and carried with it a lifetime of familiarity.

He moved rather gracefully for a large boy. Sara estimated that he had to be close to six foot tall. She guessed his age to be around sixteen or seventeen, and he looked strong, like he was used to a lot of physical activity. He looked like an average farm boy, or what she imagined one should look like.

"I am James and this is my friend, Sara," the boy answered as he eyed the delicious-smelling mixture being ladled from the pot.

"We are on our way to town. We were hoping to meet a friend of ours along the way." James paused as his stomach began to rumble loudly.

The sound made the man chuckle. He was watching Sara and James closely, almost too closely. Sara began to feel more than a little uncomfortable, like a lab rat in a controlled experiment. She turned her head slightly in his direction in order to speak, but found him staring at her with such intensity that she became nervous and forgot what she was going to say. Her mouth went dry and a small chill traveled down her spine. But then, her fears were calmed by his warm smile and a reassuring pat on her arm.

"Please excuse me," James said, his face turning a deep shade of red. "We have been traveling for a while now, and we're so hungry."

"Don't give it a second thought, young man. We're happy to share our meal with you. Now, Thomas, I'm sure they're hungrier than that. Let's not be stingy," the man said, noticing the small amount of the thick mixture the boy had put in to the bowls.

Thomas poured more stew into the bowls, and with great effort, carried them to the table. He stumbled a little and some of the stew spilled out on the floor.

"Thomas!" the man said gruffly, a heavy scowl on his face.
For a moment, it seemed to Sara that his appearance
changed a bit. There was a darkness about him, and he did
not seem so handsome.

Then she blinked, and he was smiling again, all kindness
and light.

"Here, Thomas, let me help you," the man said sweetly, as
he took the bowls from the young man and placed them in
front of Sara and James.

Sara looked questioningly at Thomas when she noticed that
his eyes were as wide as two saucers. He seemed to be
trying to tell her something, but she wasn't sure what. Sara
started to bring the spoonful of stew to her lips when,
without warning, it flew from her hand and the bowl slid
off the table of its own accord. She noticed that James's
dinner had done the same.

"Get out of here quickly!" Thomas yelled suddenly, as all
the kitchen utensils began to fly from their racks and hurl
themselves at the man.

"You will pay for this!" came the enraged cry, as the man
tried vainly to protect himself from the flying metal bowls
and pans that were hitting him. His hands flew up to cover
his head as a large mixing bowl thudded into his arm.
Automatically siding with Thomas, the three children ran
for the door and headed for the fields behind the house.
Sara and James followed behind, instinctively trusting that
Thomas was helping them. They ran until they reached a
large well at the edge of the woods, until they realized that
they could no longer move their legs. They had become
frozen to the spot. Not understanding what was happening,
Sara looked over her shoulder and saw the man leisurely
strolling up to the well, laughing at the shocked look on
their faces. "I'm so glad that you decided to stay," he said
mockingly.

"Imagine finding some of the special ones! My people will be very glad to get their hands on you. Oh, how they will reward me!"

In the middle of his self-congratulating speech their pursuer began to choke. His face was suddenly very ugly and voice shrill. Laughter turned into loud shrieks as his hair began to smoke. In vain, he tried to pat his hair, and Sara noticed that his clothing was smoking also. Apparently being on fire was extremely distracting because whatever power he had over them was vanquished. The children found that they could move now, and Sara turned to look toward the trees. The tall woman they had met them on the path earlier, the one who'd been so interested in their movements, was walking towards them. As she turned to look at Sara, she was flung to the ground and began to gasp for air. Sara turned to see that the man had gained control over whatever the woman had done to him. He was up on his feet, eyes focused on their rescuer, having a destructive effect, hurting her now.

"Stop it!" she yelled at him.

He ignored her, focusing his attention on inflicting more pain. Sara looked about her in desperation, trying to find something to help. She had to do something to stop him! Sara's anguish was so great at the woman's suffering that she barely noticed when Thomas called out to her.

"Sara, look behind you!"

When she turned towards the well again, Sara noticed that the water had risen up in a tall column that went high into the air. It seemed to be hovering, just the way it had in that abandoned house. Instinct made her focus all of her attention on the water and direct it at the man. Instantly, the water sped towards him in a rush. She thought of the hardest thing that she could, and the water turned into hail, pelting the man with such force that he was knocked out cold.

Now released, the woman began to breathe normally, and Sara sat down on the ground and cried. *What have I done? Is that man ok? More importantly, is that woman ok? Wait, should I really be worried about the man being knocked out or the fact that he could wake up any minute now and try to hurt us? This is all so confusing. I've never hurt anyone before, and he was hurting that lady. I had to do something.* All these thoughts were speeding through her head in a jumble, which only made her cry harder.

Chapter Thirteen

Sara sobbed until her nose ran and head felt awful. She cried as James and Thomas hugged her and patted her back trying to calm her down. When she finally stopped crying, Sara noticed that the man had been tied to a tree with a strange-looking cord and was still unconscious. The gray-haired woman was standing in front of her holding out a hand.

"Sara, it's getting dark now. We'd best go inside and get some rest. You still have much to do," she said firmly, as she helped Sara to her feet.

Together, they walked back towards the house. As they left the area, Sara looked back once more to see that the man was no longer visible. There was, however, what looked like ashes drifting in the breeze from the spot where he had been. It looked as if a large campfire had suddenly been extinguished and there was a rather foul, sickly sweet odor in the air that made her wrinkle her nose in disgust. She watched the ashes dance about on the wind for a minute before running back to the tree to confirm a sick suspicion she was beginning to have. The woman called out to her, but she did not stop until she was standing back in front of the tree. A crumpled pile of clothing and charred length of rope lay against the tree trunk, but there was no sign of the man. Well, actually, that wasn't true, because what was left of the man was blowing about above her head in the form of powdery soot. She watched a moment longer as the last of the ashes drifted into the sky. Then, shocked to silence, she turned and walked quickly back to the house.

The fire was still crackling merrily in the fireplace, and the house still looked homely and inviting. The only difference in the room they had left so abruptly was the vile smelling liquid that had spilled and was now eating its way through the floorboards.

"Was that the stew we were supposed to eat?" Sara asked with a look of horror on her face.

"Yes," Thomas said.

"Thank you for saving us, both of you," said James, wrinkling his nose.

"You're very welcome," the woman said softly, as she looked straight at Sara.

Sara studied her warily, wondering what was going to happen next. *Are we all going to be burnt to a crisp now? Who are you, that you are even able to do that?* The woman smiled at her as if reading her thoughts, and Sara instantly felt much safer than she had a moment before. She didn't know what made her feel that way; she just knew that it was a fact. It was as if the woman were in her mind, calming her, reassuring her. *If I wanted you gone, you would have been gone long ago on the path* came the thought out of nowhere. Sara jumped and looked at the woman with wide eyes.

"Sara, now that you are aware of what you can do, would you please clear that out for us?" said the woman calmly, as if nothing had happened.

Sara turned towards a water pump outside the door and gave the handle a good tug, then directed the trickle of water that began to flow from it towards the bubbling mess on the floor and table. The trickle of water became a heavy flow that splashed at the toxic goo and whisked it out the door.

"Who are you?" Sara asked aloud this time, turning her attention to the woman standing next to her.

"My name is Rianna. I am one of the Keepers. I am pleased to have been able to assist you today."

"What happened to that man?" Sara asked Rianna.

"He will no longer be a problem to you," she said gently. "I have to make sure you stay safe."

"Was that man your father?" Sara asked Thomas with a look of sympathy on her face.

"No. My parents were farmers who went to town the other day. They did not return. This man arrived and announced that my parents would not be back. That stranger has been in my house all this time and I could not make him leave. He acted so friendly, but all I felt when I looked at him was fear. I wanted to make him tell me where my parents were, shake it out of him. But I was too afraid to touch him. I think he knew that, and it seemed to amuse him. Beneath that pleasant exterior was evil, pure evil."

As Thomas spoke, his hands were clenched in fists and his voice became strained. Sara felt waves of guilt and shame roll off him. *I should have been able to do something. I just let him stay here! They are gone, and I did nothing.* She heard his thoughts quite clearly and looked at him sympathetically, then sent him thoughts of reassurance and comfort. He looked at her in amazement.

"Thank you," he said suddenly.

James looked at him for a moment, then nodded as if he too had shared their thoughts. Then Thomas continued to speak.

"He said that he would be staying with me until someone came to visit. He said he was here to stop something from happening. I didn't have a clue what he was talking about until you two arrived, then I knew that he meant to do something horrible to all of us. I had to stop him."

Sara received a rush of memories from Thomas as he spoke. He had two very loving adopted parents who instilled in him a love of growing things and caring for the land. Though it did not show on the surface, he mourned their loss deeply and hoped to find them soon.

"I have to prepare you three for a very dangerous mission. Haste is required now because the Garren are aware who you are and will stop at nothing to capture you. You cannot stay here. The rules must change now. You must travel tonight. Gather what supplies you can, and I will see you on your way."

While the three children hastily put food into sacks, Rianna told them of their mission to find the Healing Stone.

"The Healing Stone is an ancient object made by our creator Iam- it contains a concentrated amount of his essence- to be used only in the greatest time of need and only by those gifted enough to handle it. It is the key to fixing what has gone wrong with the balance between good and evil in this world. Good always has and always should be the dominant power. A group called the Garren has found a way to break through this pattern, and they must be stopped. The Healing Stone is in the Cold Caverns, two days' journey east from here. The stone will be closely guarded by the Gargylon, a horrible evil creature. You will have to use your wits to free the stone and deliver it to our leader Olie. He will know what to do to restore the balance. I will show you the way to start your journey. That's all that I can do, the rest of it is up to you. I will have to stay behind and make sure the Garren don't follow too closely."

Rianna herded the children out the door and walked with them to the path. Once they were on the main road, she guided them to a smaller side path that branched to the right and passed through a tall row of bushes. The path was old, narrow, and overgrown in many places. The surrounding trees made spooky shadows on the road in the fading light.

"This is the safest way to go now," said Rianna. "Move swiftly. The time is coming when we all must gather for a great battle that we cannot win if you don't complete your mission."

"Isn't it a bit late to be traveling again?" James turned to ask this all-important question but got no answer.

Rianna quickly left them as they picked their way carefully along the dark path. She moved so fast she was out of sight before they had time to register the fact that she was gone.

"She's just leaving us!" Thomas said, looking back at the now empty path.

"The Keepers have a way of doing that, and suddenly, too. No warning at all." Sara said, not bothering to look back. "In fact, this was the longest explanation I've received about why I'm here. So that's good." The troubled look her comment got from her companions compelled her to say, "But they also appear suddenly, too." As if that would provide comfort in this weird moment.

"Yes, they do. We can be thankful for that, I guess," said James.

Thomas nodded, then they continued down the path in silence for the rest of the night, afraid to make a noise, lest it attract attention.

The sun was beginning to rise slowly up over the mountaintops when the three weary travelers stumbled upon a little side path. The group stepped forward, hoping to find a place to rest. Sara was startled to find that the path widened considerably, and she soon heard the roar of a waterfall. Excited at the prospect of what they would find, Sara picked up her pace and motioned to James and Thomas to follow. Her haste was rewarded when they found themselves facing a huge waterfall. The view was breathtaking, with vivid blue water cascading down and turning into white foamy bubbles that settled into a deep pool. In front of the pool was the largest spider web Sara had ever seen. Written in the webbing were the words *Spider Falls*.

"Spider Falls." Thomas read aloud.

"Now I wonder who did that." Sara pondered staring at the elaborate message in the thread material.

"I think that should be fairly obvious," said James, pointing to the rocks surrounding the waterfall.

Sara and Thomas looked to where James was pointing and found themselves surrounded by spiders. Sara shuddered as she watched them scuttle around on their long, spindly, hairy legs. There were thousands of all sizes and colors, and all of them were ugly, and crawling towards them with great speed. A particularly large spider the size of a small horse was at the front of the advancing group. It walked straight up to Sara, and to her surprise, began to speak.

"Rianna told us to expect you," it said through lips covered with spiky hair, its fangs clacking together. "I expect that you are exhausted from your night's journey. We have prepared a resting place for you." He hissed gratingly, then turned his large head with its many eyes, indicating that they should follow him.

Sara hung back, grabbed James and Thomas's arms and urged them to stay with her.

"I don't like spiders," She whispered, "and I'm not sure they can be trusted. Maybe we should go back to the road. We've obviously wandered into the wrong place."

The children looked frantically around them for a way out of the situation. Every inch of ground was covered with spiders. Sweat trickled down their faces as they inched slowly back toward the entrance to the falls, the spiders following every move they made. As soon as a path was made, the many-legged beings scurried behind them to block the exit.

"I'm guessing they don't want us to leave," Thomas said, gripping James and Sara's hands tightly.

"Maybe we should see what they want us to do," James said, flexing his hand as it went numb beneath Thomas' strong grip. "I don't think they're going to let us out of here anyway," He observed, as the spiders moved in closer with each step the children made.

"Wait, what if this is a trick?" she whispered softly.

The largest spider turned back to the children and spoke, "If this were a trick, I assure you that the three of you would have all been quickly subdued and in a tight wrapping by now." He hissed. "We have a vested interest in seeing that you accomplish your mission. You are just as important to us as you are to the Keepers. Now if you please…" he said as he turned to walk away, indicating, once again, that they go after him.

The three children hesitated before realizing the futility of resisting, and followed the large spider to a grove of trees. Hanging down close to the ground were three large cocoons. They were tightly woven with hundreds of fine threads and lined with leaves. The outside of the cocoons was covered with a light coating of dew, which sparkled like diamonds. A fine layer of dust in the air glowed a golden color in the sunlight, giving the whole place a dreamlike quality that fascinated Sara despite her obvious dislike of its inhabitants. There was just enough of an opening in each cocoon for one child to get through. Sara touched the oval-shaped bed curiously, running her fingers over the sticky material. Her fingers came back damp but left no marks on the small pod. It swung slightly from her touch where it was suspended from a large tree.

Curiosity overcoming disgust, she looked cautiously into the narrow opening and found the inside was packed with what looked like leaves covered by more of the sticky webbing. The construction materials made the interior warm, but not hot, and looked quite comfortable.

Exhausted from the horrid experiences she'd had today, she hated the idea of crawling into an enclosed space made by gross creatures that hunted flies and could bite people and rot their flesh. How in the world was she supposed to just crawl into that potential death trap and go to sleep?

Her companions, though aware of how she felt, did not seem to be the least bit worried about being killed by their hosts. In fact, she heard them arguing about which cocoon was their's. *Seriously, Sara, I can sense they mean us no harm.* James spoke in her head so the spiders couldn't hear. *Like you sensed that man back there was trying to poison us?* Sara answered before she could stop herself. *Not fair. I was tired and I thought he was Thomas's Dad.* The slightly miffed reply came back into her head. *Sorry, you're right. I'm just a little scared.* Patting his arm to show him she really was, Sara turned to look at the cocoon once again. *If it matters, I think they're okay, too.* Thomas added his voice to James's, like talking to spiders and sleeping in cocoons was something they had done a million times before.

She was worried that they had accepted this too easily, but then again, they were also far more familiar with the gifts they possessed, using them effortlessly. What was considered magic or unusual was woven through their lives like a birthright they had accepted long ago. Maybe the whole talking insect thing was normal for this place. *I don't think we'd get very far if we tried to escape, and you heard the big guy – if they'd have wanted to hurt us they would have done so by now. Let's just stay the night and let them protect us while we sleep. I'm exhausted.* Sara cast one last look at both the boys and smiled half-heartedly to show she trusted them enough to climb in that thing. *I sure hope I don't wind up spider meat*, she added before she could help it. Not sure how to take the amused silence that followed. With a nod to each of them, she crawled into her makeshift bed, and lay there awhile listening for the sound of approaching spiders. Prepared to run for her life should the need arise- but after a time of nothing but silence- her body relaxed and she fell fast asleep.

Chapter Fourteen

Sara awoke in her unusual sleeping chamber feeling very rested, stretched her legs and pushed her feet against the flexible webbing; it expanded slowly and snapped back into place. *That's kinda neat*, she thought, pushing her feet against the stretchy net a few more times. The cocoon swayed with her movements. It was soothing and gave her time to think about the fate of her companions. Deciding to brave the presence of the spiders, she poked her head through the narrow opening to find that it was once again night. James and Thomas were sitting next to the pond eating something. Seeing that she was awake, they smiled and waved her towards them.

"We were going to wake you, but Mahew told us to let you rest a little longer." James smiled sheepishly, offering her some dried fruit.

"Mahew?" Sara said with a puzzled look.

"Mahew is the largest spider. He was the one who talked to us when we first got here. I guess you could call him their leader," said Thomas. "The spiders are working with the Keepers to defeat the Garren. When the Garren turn people evil, they destroy things, plants and animals alike. They want to help us stop this and find the Healing Stone that Rianna told us about. It will help get rid of the Garren and they will be happy with that. They're going to show us how to reach the Cold Caverns."

Sara heard the sound of leaves scrunching behind them. She turned to see the spider named Mahew, with his coarse hair and long fangs with gooey spider spit dripping from them. His appearance made her shudder and silently gag.

"I am glad to see you looking so rested," the spider said in his raspy voice. "We must begin the journey to the Cold Caverns soon. If you would like to freshen up, you should do it now."

97

"Thank you," she mumbled, turning away, unable to bring herself to face him for long.

She couldn't remember the last time she'd cleaned up properly, or be sure that she smelled very good right now. Rather than face the large spider again, she spoke to the boys, knowing it was rude but feeling it was less rude than showing her distaste. This was out of character. She was better than that, but talking to spiders! It would take time.

"I really need to clean up," she said, looking only at the boys.

"About time you did!" cried Thomas, trying to lighten the mood, splashing her with a handful of cool water from the pond.

Sara squealed, then started a water fight, which considering her special gift, she won easily. Letting her instincts take over, she manipulated the fluid substance with a growing confidence, and was able to move the water around every object the boys hid behind. Her human combatants got in a few good splashes, but all in all, they were far wetter than she.

Mahew, having always been nearby, approached them once more and said, "It will be difficult for you to travel this way."

"I know," said Sara, looking ruefully at her their clothing. She spoke again, still avoiding meeting the spider's many eyes. "I'm sorry. I guess we weren't thinking."

"I think there's some clothing in our refuse pile that you can use," said Mahew, pointing to a large pile of what looked like leaves and strips of cloth at the edge of the clearing.

The children, relieved at the chance to change their smelly and now wet clothes, ran over to examine the pile, not thinking to ask why the spiders would have clothing in their garbage where it would be quickly tainted with the stench of rotten things. Avoiding looking directly at the pile, Sara, James, and Thomas headed straight for the scraps of cloth visible on the edge of the garbage dump, hoping what they found would not smell as bad as whatever was lying around it. The trio was surprised to find several pairs of pants and shirts of various sizes strewn around this remote area. The clothing was in relatively good shape; in fact, it looked as if it had not lain outside for very long. Pulling the clothing out onto a grassy area, Sara stopped abruptly when she noticed the long, thin, white object protruding from the leg of one of the pants.

"What is that? Is that a bone!" she shrieked, seeing the familiar shape and, dropping the pants to the ground.

"I believe it is," said Thomas, bending to look at the bone as it gleamed a dull white in the moonlight. "It must be a leg bone." He shrugged at Sara's questioning look." Well, it did fall out of the pants."

The three children stopped and turned to look at the spiders who were standing in a semi-circle watching them carefully.

"You eat people?" Sara gasped, backing carefully toward the water.

Thomas and James positioned themselves protectively in front of her as the spiders began to move closer and closer. Mahew advanced slowly towards them, speaking in the same calm tone he always did.

"There have been several advance scouts for the Garren. You understand that we cannot allow them to run loose in our woods. We had to eliminate them and do not regret it.

We will not harm you. We understand your importance in freeing us all from the Garren."

As he said this, Sara could not help but wonder if this was the only reason they would not wind up as a pile of bones in the refuse pile, and didn't like the uncertainty of their situation. James paused before placing his flute, the one item he had managed to hold onto from his home, to his lips. He was ready to use its powerful effect to help them escape. This instrument had proved useful in soothing and subduing those around him. Managing a crowd of spiders would not be possible with sight alone, perhaps his music would stall them and give his friends the chance to get away.

"Do you think we can trust them?" James asked, his fingers gripping the pipe in preparation to play for his life.

"They haven't tried to hurt us yet, and they've had plenty of chances," Thomas pointed out.

"But they eat people!" Sara said, pointing back to the bones.

"They eat bad people," Thomas stated in a matter of fact tone. "We have to trust them. It's either that or hope that James can play his flute for the very long time it's going to take to get away from them."

"I guess we have no choice. But if we're going to go with them to the caverns, we'd better start now. I want to be rid of them as soon as we can," Sara said, shivering.

Nodding, James and Thomas followed her back towards the gathered spiders, the clothing from the gruesome pile still clutched in their hands. They rushed to hide behind some bushes to change. Adjusting the shirts and pants to fit, Thomas and James, rolled up their sleeves while Sara threaded a piece of fabric through the belt loop of her slightly stained, baggy pants to keep them from falling off.

Looking very much like orphans in borrowed clothes, the scared humans faced their enormous many-eyed audience. "We are ready to leave now," Sara said. "We would like to get to the caverns as quickly as we can and get this over with."

"That is very brave of you," Mahew rasped. "But you realize that even if you are able to recover the Healing Stone, it will be the beginning of your mission, not the end."

They nodded dully, not truly comprehending what was awaiting them, but afraid to ask what he meant. The three largest spiders advanced, gesturing for the children to climb on their backs. They did do reluctantly, and set off to fulfill their destiny at a much faster pace than they could on their own.

It was a two-day journey from Spider Falls to the Cold Caverns, a journey made easier by the assistance of the spiders. Despite the distrust with which she now viewed them, Sara knew that it would have taken a considerably longer time to reach their destination on foot. The spiders were able to climb easily over many obstacles that would have caused them much delay. Fallen trees, rocky terrain, boggy ground, all covered by the arachnids much faster than the two-legged creatures ever could. But, still, Sara was not happy with having to sit on the stiff, bristly backs of these huge man-eating creatures that could easily turn and devour all three of them in a split-second.

Though not exactly sure where the Cold Caverns were, they all seemed to know when they were getting close. The feeling of dread they had when starting this important journey got stronger and stronger with each step the spiders took.

The theory of becoming heroes fighting to save lots of people suddenly became very real and frightening. Sara was beginning to get the feeling that she hadn't quite grasped the significance of what she might have to do to accomplish the task – none of them had. By the time this realization had truly hit her, it was too late. The spiders had come to a stop in front of a large black hole in the side of a mountain. Puffs of icy air wafted from the opening with a force strong enough to blow the hair back from their faces. Sara shivered and took a deep breath, barely noticing that the spiders, without so much as a goodbye or good luck wish, had turned and scampered out of sight. The message was clear: they had reached their destination and were expected to complete their mission on their own. It was now or never: they had to enter.

Chapter Fifteen

The stunned travelers faced the opening which appeared to descend into total darkness. The closer they got, the stronger the frigid gusts of air became. Sara backed away, rubbing at the goose bumps that rose on her arms. It didn't give her much confidence to see her companions standing just as indecisively, not any more eager to enter than she was. *How are we going to find our way through that?* she thought bleakly. Looking around for some kind of inspiration, she spotted a small pond to the side of the entrance. Sunlight reflected on its surface and gave her an idea. Concentrating on the surface of the water, Sara formed several softball-sized orbs and levitated them into the air, noting with satisfaction that the sunlight remained captured in the water and could provide a satisfactory light source if she could just hold their shape.

"Wow," Thomas and James said in unison when they saw what she had done.

They crossed under the orbs and looked at them with awe. Thomas reached up and tapped one lightly with his finger; the shape held as it bounced away from him.

"That's wonderful, Sara," he said, admiringly.

Sara beamed at the praise, surprised at how quickly she was mastering her new skill. Smiling, she began to move the orbs slowly around in a circle, concentrating on keeping the shape of the water. While she was playing with the water, a sharp blast of cold air whipped her cheek. Her smile dimmed when she turned once more in the direction of the cave and realized that they would now have to enter, battle a horrible monster for the Healing Stone, and come back out into a world filled with all kinds of bad guys who wanted to hurt them, then find a way to get it to Olie, wherever he was, in order to stop all of this madness.

And what if there were more to it, more enemies, more missions; more problems? Remembering what Mayhew had said, she wished she'd been brave enough to ask him some questions. Why did everyone assume they knew all the important stuff and were good to go ahead with this dangerous mission?

"I don't know if I can handle this," she said, suddenly feeling overwhelmed.

"We can handle this," Thomas said firmly, taking her hand. She was startled to feel him trembling, despite his calm tone.

"There's something bad down there," she said softly. "Maybe we don't have to do this."

Thomas's eyes brightened for a moment. "Yeah, maybe there's another way," he said hopefully.

"What is it?" James piped in from behind them. "The other way?" He looked with dread in the direction of the cave, a fine sheen of sweat formed on his forehead.

They sat down outside the cave and thought for a long time about possible alternatives to this risky venture.

"We need that stone, don't we?" Thomas asked finally, when no one came up with a suggestion.

"Things are no good without it, right? Is this the only place to get a Healing Stone? Maybe there are more stones, someplace else."

"I don't think it's that easy," she said, frowning. "If there were others available, then everyone would have access to them, and that means the Garren would have them, too. And this whole thing wouldn't be happening. It has to be the only one."

Thomas was holding a small stone in his hand and threw it onto the ground in frustration. "We have to go in there! How fair is it? We're kids, for goodness sake! Shouldn't the grown-ups be doing this?" The children looked at each other mutely. In their hearts, they knew this conversation was all just a big stall tactic. They were meant to do this and would have to go into the darkness and face whatever was down there. It was the only way.

"Maybe I can go alone," Sara whispered so softly, they could barely hear her. "You wouldn't be doing this if I hadn't shown up on your doorstep." She looked at James as she spoke. Her lips felt numb as the words left her mouth, an ice cold sweat formed on her face.

"No, you can't," James said sternly. "We would not be here if there was another way, and we're not just any children. We can do things that others can't. That's got to mean something. There must be hope of our coming out of there."

With this thought, Sara got up the courage to step up to the mouth of the cave and look back at the boys. Thomas moved to stand beside her and looked back at James, who in turn stepped resolutely up beside them and gripped Sara's hand. Taking one last look over their shoulders, the three children slowly entered the cave, the glowing water globes bobbing in the air ahead of them.

Shivering from the cold draft that hit them, they steadfastly moved forward on shaky legs. In the weak light of her water globes, a straight path could be seen running through the rocky walls that sloped downward. Having no choice but to continue, they followed the path, moving around the occasional large boulder, avoiding cracks and sudden dips in the ground. Most of the cave was in total darkness. Sara was only able to keep the immediate path in front of them lit with her water globes, and it was proving to be a challenge. The cold breeze that blew through the cave bounced the globes around, and she had to constantly focus her energy to move them back in line. What she could see in the dim light was not particularly impressive. There were dark, moss-covered rocks and a few rock formations hanging from the ceiling.

Distracted by maintaining the only light source in this very dark place, she was counting on James and Thomas to physically guide her along the path. The children held hands to prevent being separated and continued to head downward. The cave was so cold they could see the faint white mist of their breath hanging in the air in front of them and their skin was again covered with goose bumps. Sara was forced to stop suddenly when they came to a fork in the path. She was sandwiched between the two boys, her abrupt halt caused them to bump into her from both sides.

"Sorry," they both said as they gathered themselves together, steadying Sara before she fell.

"Which way do we go from here?" Thomas asked, looking from one dark hole to the other.

"I don't know," Sara said with a little wail, her voice echoing in the wide cavern.

"We're looking for the Healing Stone, right?" James said.

"Of course we are," said Sara and Thomas together.

"What color is it supposed to be?" James asked.

"I'm not exactly sure," Sara said. "But I had a dream once, and it had red stones in it." "Well, that settles it then," James said, pointing to the left. "We go that way."

"How did you decide that?" Thomas asked, puzzled by his sudden decision.

Taking Thomas by the shoulders, James turned him to the left branch of the path. There was a faint red glow coming from that direction.

"I guess that settles it, then. We go that way," James said, but he didn't move. None of them did.

"We really should be going," Sara said softly, but stayed where she was.

"I guess that's what we should do," agreed Thomas, blowing out frosty puffs of air, not budging an inch.

"Of course," said James. "We all know that there is some kind of monster waiting down there. Don't you think it would be good to have some sort of plan?"

"A plan sounds sensible. I've never really had to deal with a monster before. How do you handle one?" Sara asked, turning toward James.

"We have to find out what its weaknesses are, then attack them," Thomas piped in, but it sounded more like a question than a definitive statement.

"Ok, how do we find out what its weaknesses are?" Sara asked.

"Umm, maybe since it lives in a cave, it can't stand light," James said with sudden conviction.

"That's hardly a problem; look, we have light sources here." Thomas pointed to the water globes.

"Somehow, I don't see these as being a threat to it," Sara said, looking at the weak light emitting from the suspended globes.

"There has been enough light coming from these to get us through this cave so far, and it's pretty dark in here," Thomas said, pointing to the pitch-black interior of the cave beyond the light sources.

"Then there's always your flute," Sara said to James. "You know what happens when you play."

"You can mesmerize it," Thomas agreed.

"I hope I can," James murmured. "I've never tried it on a monster before."

"You can bring the stone to us, Thomas," Sara said, suddenly hopeful that they would be spared the trip down to where the Gargylon waited. Because one of the few things that she was certain of was that it was waiting for them. There would be no surprise on their part.

"Only if I can get close enough to it," Thomas said. "I cannot move things from too great a distance. I'm sorry, Sara." A look of sorrow crossed his face, knowing that his limitations would cause them to have to face the thing down below.

She smiled at him and tried not to show her disappointment at having to travel further.

"I'm sorry to have upset you, Thomas. I guess we should have known that this whole trip wasn't going to be easy." She hugged him tightly and turned toward the passage with a look of determination.

"We have a plan now," James said. "I guess that means we have to go down there. Right?"

"Right," Thomas and Sara said together. They tried to inject some confidence into their voices, but barely managed to squeak out the word.

Together they headed downward, following the red light, which got brighter with every step they took. The air seemed to grow thicker and warmer as they neared their destination. The walls of the cave were closing in a bit, too. They had to travel single file now, each one holding on to the shirt of the one in front in order to stay near to each other. The walls were so close now that Sara could feel the brush of stone on her sleeve. When she pulled her arm close to her side, it felt damp. She was surprised to find that both her arm and her hand glowed brightly where the slimy stuff had gotten on her.

"Phosphorous!" she exclaimed.

James and Thomas stopped to look questioningly at Sara as she pointed excitedly to the rocks around them.

"What is it?" James asked from the front of the line.

"Phosphorous," Sara repeated.

"Oh, I've heard of that stuff," Thomas piped in. "It lights things up, right?"

"Oh, yeah!" James looked on in wonder at the sides of the cave, beginning to understand her excitement.

"It's coming from the rocks." She held her glowing hand up for the boys to see. "Rub your hands on the rock, then all over your clothes and skin."

Without questioning her, the boys did what she said. Soon, they all had a noticeable white glow about their bodies.

"Just in case something happens to the lights," Sara explained, "I don't want us to lose each other."

Nodding solemnly, the three glowing bodies continued down the narrow passageway, again stopping suddenly when James tumbled headfirst into a wide chamber, his fall stopped by the sharp tug that Thomas gave to his shirt. The startled young man stepped back to huddle with Sara and Thomas as they looked cautiously around in the muted light. The small crew was fairly certain that they were safe for the moment. The ground in their immediate area was relatively flat, except for the steep decline they had just encountered, all else was worn stone and some projections from above and below.

The cavern was huge but they couldn't see much beyond the faint globes of light bobbing around above them and their own illuminated bodies. Each step still had to be carefully taken to avoid injury or sudden death. Though the direction of travel had been made clearer by the red light shining faintly but teasingly in the distance, no one moved for a minute or two. Sara noticed with dismay that when the echoes from their footsteps had ceased, she had begun to hear another faint echoing noise, making her skin crawl as she stood perfectly still in this seemingly endless cavern. They weren't here alone; something else was walking– scrape, tap, scrape, tap. Why was she surprised by this? There was no way that they could expect to waltz in and take the Healing Stone out of here. There was going to be some kind of fight and they weren't trained warriors. Despite the cold, she felt a fine sheen of perspiration on her forehead, and thought again of the obvious question: How do you fight a monster? The trio stood listening for the scuffling they heard before, but there was just a steady dripping of water as it fell from somewhere up above to land with a plop on the rocks around them. Something evil shared this space with them, tainting the air, turning it foul and making it difficult to breathe. She could tell that the others sensed it too; felt their fear, heard their ragged breathing as they moved further into the cavern. The air was moving freely around them in the wide-open space they now occupied. In fact, it was moving so freely that Sara temporarily lost control of the water-filled light globes. They bounced wildly around; one of them burst as it hit a large rock formation, splattering water on the walls. Worried about the loss of one of their meager light sources, Sara focused all of her attention on the remaining globes, gathering them to the area just in front of her, ruing her carelessness. Then she saw it; glowing faintly up ahead, a bright-red stone sitting atop a large pile of rocks. Thinking only of reaching this much talked about object, she headed straight for it, her companions hot on her heels. All thoughts of immediate danger gone; she just wanted to grab the thing and get out of this place. *Maybe we can get it and just leave before anything else happens. Maybe this won't be so bad.* But haste makes for careless behavior. They really should have been paying attention. What happened next made that abundantly clear.

A sound stopped her in her tracks, more scraping against the rocks, as if something sharp were being dragged across them, followed by a rasping noise, like a scaly fish flopping around on a hard surface. The air around her got even colder. She looked down to see that her fingertips had turned blue and she began shivering so hard that she lost all control of the water globes. The watery orbs, which now resembled large glass light bulbs, had started to freeze at the further drop in temperature. Soon the globes fell crashing to the cave floor, breaking into several pieces. The only lights in the cave now came from the Healing Stone and the faint glow of their bodies from the phosphorous. Thankfully, it was bright enough to keep the darkness from overwhelming them but revealed little else than what was in their immediate area.

And still she heard the furtive noises coming closer and closer – scrape, tap, scrape, tap – and was that a low growl? Sara cautiously turned her head in the direction of the disturbing sounds. From out of the shadows, a ghostly figure emerged. Mouth dry from shock, she stared at the creature. Standing before her was a beast unlike anything she had encountered before. A cross between a large man and a lizard, it stood before her on two feet with the sharpest claws she had ever seen. It was so thin; its ribs stuck out prominently, its skin was stretched tightly over its body like plastic wrap over leftovers, except this plastic wrap was covered in scaly flesh and had a tail that scraped against the floor when it moved. This thing had the brightest green eyes she had ever seen, and they were looking directly at her with disturbing intensity. It smiled, flashing razor sharp teeth. That smile had nothing to do with friendliness; it was a smile of pure evil. The brief acknowledgment of the children's presence was the only warning.

The creature jumped at her, sharp claws extended, ready to strike. Flinging herself backward to avoid contact, Sara was surprised when the Gargylon stopped mid–leap, falling back to the floor when a large rock sailed from the left and struck its head. She soon learned that Thomas was throwing rocks at the Gargylon, and his aim was excellent. Seeking to protect his friend, he kept up the attack until the monster rolled onto the floor, stunned by the impact. Quickly recovering, it started to rise again, only for James to overcome his shock and begin to play his flute. At first, the sound seemed to confuse the Gargylon. It continued to slowly advance towards Sara, shaking its head as if to dismiss the sound. Then it stumbled again. Eye growing heavy, the creature stared at her through half-closed lids. Its green eyes still alert, but dazed. Taking advantage of the monster's distress, Sara turned toward Thomas and pointed to the Healing Stone which the creature was standing right in front of. She would have to pass that thing to reach it and she really didn't want to.

"Hurry!" she yelled. "Let's get the stone and get out of here! Can you bring it to us?"

Thomas turned towards the stone and concentrated. It was still far enough away to take some time to get to. He focused all of his energy on moving it toward Sara, but it wouldn't budge. After several minutes of trying, he turned to Sara with a puzzled look.

"I can't move it. This has never happened to me before."

James, trying to keep the Gargylon mesmerized, continued to play, but he was beginning to get a little winded. The notes fell flat before he was able to catch his breath and continue.

In the pause between notes, Sara was sure that she saw the Gargylon blink, as if the spell cast by the music had been broken for just that instant. Sara knew that James could not keep this up much longer, and when the creature regained its wits, they were going to be in big trouble. Being the closest to both the stone and the monster, Sara skirted carefully past its emaciated body and desperately ran to the niche where the stone was housed. Scrambling up a pile of rocks, she grabbed the Healing Stone, scraping her hands and knees as she did. Much to her surprise, it came off easily when she pulled it down.

"We've got to get out of here," she cried, running towards Thomas, the stone clasped tightly in her hand, gesturing towards James to follow them as they headed back toward the path.

James stumbled after them. Trying to play his flute while running proved to be too difficult. He was forced to stop just as he reached the path and navigate the uneven floor with care. As soon as he stopped, the Gargylon began to move its head from side to side until it had sighted them once again. Now free from the effects of James's hypnotic spell, it began to stumble in their direction, thin legs picking up speed as the magic of the music faded. Sara reached the path first and, quickly turning, pushed Thomas then James toward the thin path that lead out of the cavern. The panicked trio was guided through the rocky terrain by the light of the Healing Stone, which Sara held in front of her.

Not daring to slow down, they made their way towards the exit, all too aware that the Gargylon was close behind and gaining ground fast. Sara could hear it thumping clumsily against the stones behind them, knocking rocks loose as it charged up the path. Its shrill shrieking cry echoing in the cave around them seemed to come from everywhere. Then, suddenly, there was silence. Though they continued to clamber upward, following the single path that had led them to the stone, Sara no longer heard the frantic scrambling behind them. For some reason, rather than be comforted by this, she was worried. *There's no way it's just given up*, she thought, as she stopped abruptly to listen carefully for sounds of continued pursuit. She heard nothing, but she just knew it was close, could still feel its oily presence. *Where are you?* Breathing heavily, they knew they weren't out of danger. They had now reached the fork in the path. James pointed to the right.

"This is the way we came. We just need to go back this way, and then we can get out of here."

Elated at the possibility of completing the mission and getting back to his family, he turned to run through the opening, only to find himself face to face with the Gargylon! The creature was slowly lowering itself from the rock wall. It had followed them by crawling on the roof of the cave.

Its eyes were full of cunning as it made its way toward James. Strong arms whipped out, claws caught James's shirt and pulled him toward it.

"Jamessss," the creature hissed as its bony fingers tightened their grip on his clothing.

Sara felt all of the blood drain from her face. It knew their names! As if reading her thoughts, the creature turned to look directly at her.

"Sara," it said, a gurgling laugh coming from between its thin black lips. Then, smiling at her, the creature raised its other arm to strike James down.

All the while, it continued to watch her as if enjoying the horrified expression on her face. When the sharp claws were about to meet his face, James's foot hit a slick spot, and he fell backwards onto the cave floor. The creature was forced to let go to avoid falling with him. With James now free, Thomas began to fling every loose stone he could find at the creature. The Gargylon reeled from the impact, but continued to advance towards James.

Quickly gathering his wits, he began to play his flute again. Like before, the monster slowed its pace and stood entranced by the sound while Thomas continued to place rock after rock over it. Soon the pile of rocks completely covered the monster, and it moved no more. With escape once again possible, the youngsters hurriedly moved away from the pile of rocks and continued to move upward until they could once again see sunlight streaming from the entrance of the cave. *A few more steps and we will be safe*, Sara thought. Unfortunately, she was wrong.

Chapter Sixteen

They stumbled into the warm sunlight and sat on the ground, relieved to be alive. It felt wonderful to thaw out. Shivering, they watched their skin take on a flesh-colored hue having lost that bluish tint from their time in the cave. Sara sat next to James, carefully checking his arms for scrapes and cuts. Patting her hand impatiently, he assured that he really wasn't hurt.

They remained there for a while, thinking about their next move. For all the importance that had been attached to this magical stone, now they had it and had no idea what to do with it. Sara held up the Healing Stone and studied it carefully. The stone was roughly the size of a tennis ball with several angles cut into it that seemed to capture the sunlight, reflecting its bright-red color on the ground around them. It was very light, yet seemed to vibrate from within as if a great force were straining to be released.

"Now that we have the stone, what are we supposed to do with it?" Thomas asked, voicing Sara's thoughts.

"We have to get it to Olie," Sara said, remembering the plan from when she'd first learned what was expected of her.

"Yes, I believe I heard that before," Thomas said in an exasperated tone. "But I don't believe that anyone ever said exactly where he was located and how we're supposed to get there."

Sara was about to answer Thomas with what she hoped was an encouraging speech when a movement in the bushes around them caught her attention. Hurriedly rising, Sara swung round, but now the sound was coming from several directions, not just one. Leaves rustling, swaying greenery, followed by a faint giggling noise. As close as they were, her alarm was their alarm, and Thomas and James jumped up to their feet with their backs to her so they face outward in a circle, ready to defend themselves. The cause of their combined unease was soon revealed. The bushes parted all around them and out stepped ten extremely thin women with wild black and red hair streaming in long masses all around them. Their hair was in constant motion, as if a current of air was blowing it upwards. Their faces, brown and wrinkled, resembled animated tree bark, creaking with each change of expression. The long, dark gowns they wore flowed around them as they moved steadily toward the three children. As they moved, they let out a strange shrill laugh that Sara found hauntingly familiar. Lem had mentioned these things- and she had heard them but not seen them. Now she was wishing she didn't have to. "Hateresses!" she cried.

"They are the Garren's hunters!" Thomas and James backed closer together, ready to be attacked at any moment.

Thomas turned his head and directed several tree branches at the Hateresses, who knocked the branches aside with a flick of their wrists. Sneering at him, they continued to advance. Sara, using her only defense, gathered all the water from the pond and sent it streaming straight at the Hateresses. This seemed to have more of an effect, it drove them backwards, but not for long; they gathered themselves and began to advance towards the children once more. James started to play his flute, which only seemed to make them move in slow motion, and they began to wail loudly to drown out the sound of his music. Due to his lack of success, he stopped playing and turned towards his friends with a look of despair. The children prepared themselves for the inevitable assault, clutching each other's hands and huddling closer together. As their hands touched the stone, they began to glow brightly. She felt a tremendous heat spread through her that was passed to the others. The first

Hateress to reach them grasped Sara by the arm and melted instantly on the spot. Several others met a similar fate as they attempted to grab the boys. The enraged cries of the Hateresses filled the air as they failed to harm the children. They hovered nearby, unable to come too close but unwilling to leave until they found a way to get to their intended victims.

Yet another of the evil creatures approached, standing very close to Sara, so close that she could feel its breath which smelled like kerosene and rotted wood. This time, it did not touch her, just hung there and stared. She looked back defiantly and felt herself drawn in to those empty black eyes, unable to look away. What she saw made her blood run cold. She saw misery and certain death for them all. *Give up, you will all die* was the message in her head. *We will win anyway and this will all have been for nothing*.

She continued to watch in horrified fascination as Thomas and James were pulled away from her, and one by one, the life force left their bodies in a thin golden stream, until all that was left was a shriveled shell. The husks of their bodies sat on the ground unmoving.

Shocked and saddened by the loss of her two best friends, she reached out to them to try to help, but something was holding her back. Startled, she felt a sharp tug on her hand and found herself standing next to Thomas once again. He was holding her hand in a crushing grip, which he relaxed as soon as he was aware she was focused on him.

"You almost let go of my hand. You were reaching for the Hateress. Don't look at her anymore. I think she was hypnotizing you or something" Thomas squeezed her hand again. She felt the Healing Stone press into her palm. Its warmth gave her comfort and renewed confidence.

An enraged shriek came from the Hateress directly in front of her, it reached out and tried to rake its fingers down her face, only to be burned up as soon as a cold finger touched her skin. Sara expected to see the Hateresses take to their heels and abandon the effort when they realized they could not get to them. She was surprised to see that this did not happen. Instead of leaving, the Hateresses pulled back into a circle and waited.

"What are they doing?" James asked. His question seemed to amuse the Hateresses, for they cackled merrily at him and stood in the circle, looking at them with burning dark eyes.

It wasn't long before they heard the noise of a large group approaching through the woods.

"It must be the Garren!" Sara cried in despair. "They must have let them know we are here somehow!"

The Hateresses got louder, hissing and laughing, turning towards the woods. Their look of triumph soon faded when the group that burst through the trees turned out to be a large group of spiders traveling at full speed. The spiders were everywhere, dropping from trees and covering every inch of exposed ground between the Hateresses and the children. The Hateresses swatted wildly at their clothing as spiders began to climb up their long robes. Within seconds, the larger spiders were able to drag the Hateresses into the bushes while the little ones nibbled on the exposed skin of their arms.

"Perhaps you should leave now," Mahew said as he emerged from the bushes behind his spider army. "This will not be pleasant, and the Garren really are on their way. The battle has begun. It is being fought all over this land now. Your journey must be completed at all costs."

Without having to be told twice, the children turned to run in the only clear direction left to them, a small path made by the spiders leading away from the ugliness taking place there. They walked towards the forest, uncertain of their destination beyond merely escaping the area. As they entered the wood, Sara was stopped suddenly by a hand on her shoulder. She jumped backwards ready to run as fast as she could, the thought of getting away overriding concern for where she went. But when she looked up, she saw a familiar round face with wispy gray hair smiling down on her.

"Ferd!" she cried excitedly and leaned in to give the big man a relieved hug. Though having met just once, she felt better knowing he was here to save the day. He must have brought the spiders to their rescue.

"Glad to see you made it out alright, girl," he smiled, returning her hug. "You found the other two and the stone so quickly! I knew you would do well." He patted her back gently while glancing behind her. "Now would be a good time to get you three away from here, I think," he said, bringing her attention back to the fighting behind them.

With casual and feigned unconcern, Ferd took Sara's hand and led her in a straight path away from the scene of violence. The boys followed closely, hand in hand. Thomas clutched Sara's shirttail, too afraid of the twists and turns their day had taken to lose contact with her for even one second. It was an awkward way to travel, but it was better than being separated, so they walked for a while in this manner, not stopping until they reached a flat treeless area several miles away from the caverns. The clearing was a small one shaded by many large trees. Ferd waved his hand and offered them a seat on some conveniently located tree stumps and began to talk as if his audience hadn't just run away from some very ugly and scary beings, like it was an everyday occurrence.

"I will waste little time," he said. "The battles have already begun, and everyone is needed to fight the evil forces of the Garren. Olie is now on the Island of Hope. You will have to get to him quickly. He has survived an attack by the Garren's most bloodthirsty forces but is gravely injured. He is holding them back with his superior mind control, feeding them images of large dragons and sea monsters. This cannot last long, as his strength is fading. If they are able to get to him, then it will all be over. All the good in this world will wither and die if Olie dies. It all starts with him. He needs you desperately. I will lead you to the vessel you must use to reach him, then I must stay behind to prevent the Garren from overtaking you." Ferd looked at each of them with a sad half smile on his face. "I'm so sorry that your young lives have been interrupted by all of this. You never had a chance at a normal childhood. That was all taken from you when your parents offered you as our saviors. They did love you, you know. Perhaps when this is all over…" He stopped abruptly, rubbing his eyes. "Did you know our parents well?" Sara asked, intrigued by the possibility of knowing where she came from, where they all came from. She had known she and James were orphans, and when she met Thomas, knew he was not a natural part of the loving family he'd lost just before meeting them. It was all part of the instant knowing they all shared. What they didn't know was anything about their lives before they wound up where they had lived most of their lives until now.

"I knew them very well. They were brave and good people. When the Garren rose up and rebelled against Olie, they chose to let the souls of the healers enter into your bodies." Ferd saw the look of distress that crossed their faces when he said this. "Please don't misunderstand; you lost nothing. You are as you were before, you just gained the powers, wisdom, and compassion of three very wonderful Keepers who were taken from this world far too early.

They were very good friends of mine, and I am happy to see that they share in your life. We did our best to see that you were protected, hidden from the Garren. We found homes for you so that you would be cared for like normal children with families. Sara, I cannot express enough my regret at the life you were given. It was so different than Thomas and James's. I know that now because I can see your memories. They had kindness and a sense of belonging while you did not. We chose to let Salius place you in homes and to keep us totally ignorant of your whereabouts because we wanted to keep you safe for as long as possible. Salius has not been seen since that time. I swear to you, Sara, we would have changed things for you if we had known." He had tears running down his face freely now.

"It's alright, really," Sara said, patting him gently on the arm, feeling worse for him at the moment than she did for herself. She no longer carried the bad memories with her. Instead she had all of Thomas and James's good memories to enjoy. They had been so happy, she felt as if she'd had a wonderful childhood along with them. And so, in typical Sara fashion, she did her best to make Ferd feel better. "Everything happens for a reason, and I feel lucky to have met Thomas and James. I know we are where we belong, doing what we were meant to do. It's all coming together now, and we must get to Olie quickly and set things right."

It all sounded so good, but they all knew she was a terrified child trying to sound brave, accompanied by two others who were as scared as she was. But like the good friends they were quickly becoming Thomas and James threw themselves into the roles of fearless warriors, ready to face more scary things with her. Though trembling inside, and fooling absolutely no one, her companions stood up and presented a united front.

"Lead on, Ferd; Olie is waiting for us," Thomas said, reaching for Sara and James's hands.

Ferd nodded solemnly, knowing they didn't really mean it and didn't truly know what they were facing. But that didn't stop him from leading them on as requested. All parties fully aware that while they were children, they were still the right people for this job. It was their destiny.

They started walking again for a long while, each caught up in their own thoughts, not really registering what they passed. It didn't matter anyway. Strangely, walking in this land was more like passing scenery in a car going fast down a road – they saw and remembered little of it. In fact, it was all a blur, faint images of trees, mountains, lakes sped by, and they weren't even walking that fast. It didn't make sense, but then again not much had made sense since she arrived here. Mile after mile of ever-changing scenery passed like a dream until finally it all became crystal-clear. Time seemed to snap back into its regular pace. Without warning, the blur became solid, three dimensional objects appearing like props dropped from the sky. At first, they stood unsteadily, having left an out of control merry-go-round to land on solid ground. The bewildered group found themselves in a grove of trees listening to the sound of waves crashing on a nearby shore.

Chapter Seventeen

Moving cautiously behind Ferd's large frame, Sara and her companions, tried to adapt to the slower pace of reality. It was several more minutes before Sara got the courage to say anything, not having been confident enough in her headlong flight to utter a word before. But now that they had stopped, she blurted out a question they all wanted answered.

"Where are we going?"

A long pause followed in which their guide stopped walking and stood perfectly still, his bulky form bending down slightly as if the weight of the world had settled on his shoulders before turning to give her the saddest look she'd ever seen.

"A place I cannot follow," he answered in the typically cryptic fashion she'd come to expect from the Keepers. Motioning gently, he indicated they follow him once more. *Why waste time with lengthy explanations when things could be found out the hard way?* Sara saw Ferd stiffen up for a second, as if her thoughts were easily read, before moving on as if he had no choice but to continue onwards. Somehow, without it ever haven been spoken aloud, she understood that there was something more to this. Ferd was answering to someone else. Olie? It might be awhile (if ever) before she would learn all she needed to know about this situation. The Keepers had a mission and she, James and Thomas were a small but important part of it. Knowing just enough would have to do for now, Sara promised herself that she would discover what was needed and be ready to protect her friends against anyone who tried to hurt them. She was a child to whom caution had always been a necessity and though her circumstances had changed, she was going to adapt and survive for all their sakes.

Once again, Ferd nodded in response to the unspoken thought without once glancing back. They moved on for a short while longer. The trees started to thin out until Sara could see sand on the forest floor and the sound of the ocean got louder and louder. Soon the group stepped out of the trees to stand on a beach that looked like a postcard. The sky was the brightest blue she had ever seen, and the shoreline seemed to stretch out in front of her for miles. The waves were lapping gently onto the sand with a steady hiss. The soothing sound made Sara aware of how tired she was. Fighting the sudden urge to lie on the beach and fall asleep, the young girl looked around her more carefully. There had to be a reason why they were here, because here didn't go any further, the long stretch of sandy beach and endless view of ocean didn't leave any further avenue for travel. So, this must be their destination.

"Well…" James started uncertainly, "what are we doing here?"

"Is Olie here?" Sara asked looking for signs of some kind of house.

"No." Ferd was watching them closely, moving his hands in an odd pattern, never once taking his eyes from the children.

Though still standing on the same beach, under the same warm sun, Sara was aware that something had changed. Thomas was the first to notice the little addition to the landscape.

"Look there!" he said, pointing to an object floating a short distance from the shore.

The group studied the object and saw that it was a boat the size of a school bus bobbing in the water. Noting with interest the bright-red hull that was suddenly visible where it hadn't been before. "There is your craft," Ferd said.

"This is where you start the last leg of your journey. Your

route has been programmed into that ship; it should take you straight to Olie. Keep in mind that Olie is still very strong despite his injuries and is able to erect barriers to keep the island safe. Some are illusions and some are real. Be careful, the barriers are not constructed to keep some out; they are constructed to keep all out. They will not just let you pass; you will have to find a way through."

"Why can't you take us to him?" Thomas voiced the question for them all.

"I am needed for other things," was the quiet reply.

And Sara knew it was the truth. Her heart went out to the Keeper who, despite her misgivings about what had not been said, genuinely cared about them and was sad to be leaving them now.

She looked at the boys and simply shook her head. They knew what she meant, what she felt, and the questions stopped because it was this collective certainty that steadied their minds.

"How are we supposed to get to the boat?" James asked.

"I'm sure Sara can help you with that," Ferd said, smiling at her.

Grateful for the opportunity to do anything but dwell on things they couldn't control, Sara turned around and concentrated on the area of the sea separating them from the boat. The sea began to part, and soon there was a strip of dry land leading to the small craft. "Good job!" cried Ferd, all the while herding them towards the boat.

Allowing herself to enjoy the praise, Sara turned back to give Ferd a hug. In return, he hugged her just as fiercely and patted the boys on the back.

"May your journey be blessed. Hurry on now, children; we will keep the Garren at bay for as long as we can."

"We?" said James, curious at the phrasing, the growing urgency coming from the formerly calm Ferd.

127

"Please, just go." He was pushing them now, no longer concerned about them picking up on his worried state. Doing as they were told, they started walking towards the boat. When they were almost there, Sara looked back once to find that Ferd was not alone on the beach. There was a long line of people standing next to him. Sara recognized Maggie as one of them. All were looking solemnly at the departing children.

"Who are they?" Thomas asked as he looked back.

"Those are the Keepers," Sara said. "And I think this is their last stand."

"Let's not let them down then," James said as they finally reached the boat.

There was a ladder dangling from the side and they climbed aboard the vessel. The boat looked old, but well-kept. Its aged wooden deck was clean, the sails had many patches in place, but looked to be in working order. After initial examination of the craft, assuring themselves it was indeed safe to navigate the open seas, they stayed on deck for a while, watching as the shoreline and the Keepers were but a mere speck visible in the distance. Each was disturbed by the thought of being sent out to face the unknown again, with the world's fate resting on their shoulders. Because there was clearly much more to all of this than just returning a stone to someone.

With nothing to look at now but miles of ocean, Sara and her companions began to explore the vessel bobbing beneath their feet. There was a small cabin topside, which, when they entered it, contained a twin bed and a desk. Upon the desk was a collection of navigational tools and a few maps that bore a fine coating of dust. The maps were yellowed with age indicating a long period of disuse and the metal tools had a red coating of rust upon them.

Wherever this boat had come from, it hadn't been used in quite some time.

"It's old," James voiced the groups concerns. "Hope it doesn't sink before we get where we're going."

Though questions were many, none were asked. It didn't seem to matter if they wanted answers if no one could provide them. Moving around seemed the best distraction. Thomas approached the desk and looked at the objects.

"Any idea how to use these things?" He picked up a compass, looking at it curiously.

"We don't have to know how," James said, trying to sound confident. "Ferd said the boat is programmed to get us there, remember?"

As if on cue, the boat started to move, slowly at first, gaining speed as the raised sails picked up the wind. Wooden masts creaked, guided by some unseen hand, directing the ship where it was supposed to go. Far enough out now that no land was visible. Everything began to look the same – water and more water. Surrounded by rolling waves so gentle it was like rocking in a cradle, they began to get very sleepy. After a quick meal of dried fruit from their packs, the children retired to the cabin. The boys let Sara use the bed while they found two hammocks rolled up in a chest and strung them up on the braces in the center of the cabin. Exhausted by the battle with the Gargylon and constant traveling, the adventurers slept for some time.

They woke to feel the boat rocking wildly about. Jumping up quickly as they could, they grabbed at the sparse furnishings as the boat lurched sickeningly around them. Luckily, the furniture was bolted securely to the floor or they would have had a hard time maintaining control over their movements. Sara made it to the cabin door first-flung it open and was immediately hit in the face with a spray of salty water. Staggering out onto the deck, she concentrated on the sea around the boat. As soon as she thought about it being calm, the sea around them began to settle down to a gentle roll. Sara noted the lack of activity elsewhere. The sky above was blue and cloudless, with no indication of a storm.

"We must be getting close. Ferd did say he'd be warning us off."

"Then it's only going to get worse, isn't it?" James said grimly, scanning the area around the boat for signs of what might be coming next.

It wasn't long before they found out. The stillness of the air was broken by a loud, piercing shriek followed by a sudden rush of air as a large animal swooped down from the sky towards them. The creature reminded Sara of a picture she had seen of a prehistoric bird in her school textbook called a Pterodactyl. It was flying down towards their little craft, its beak open and claws extended as it sped straight at her. Its large wings moved the air all around the boat, causing the waves to hit the hull with renewed force, sending water sloshing onto the deck. James pulled his flute from his pocket and began to play as the Pterodactyl flew within a few feet. The music had no effect on the animal.

"It can't be real," Thomas said, noting the lack of reaction it had to James's music.

"What do you mean not real," Sara shrieked, looking at him as if he had lost his mind.

"That imaginary thing sure is causing quite an air current!"

"It's not real," Thomas repeated. "Every living thing is affected by James's music. This thing is not alive! James, play again," he said, ducking to avoid the rigging, as it was forced back toward him by the wind.

James began to play, as the Pterodactyl swung around to make another dive for the boat. He blew into the

130

instrument; the haunting melody hung in the air, but had no effect on the animal whatsoever.

"See," Thomas said, "it's not real. This Olie is powerful, right? Remember what Ferd said. He can create illusions to protect himself. Think of it as not real."

They stood together holding hands and thought of it as not real as it swooped past their heads letting out a piercing caw. Now that the group had determined to consider this a non-threat, they shared this thought and stood their ground. Disbelief caused the flying dinosaur to shimmer in and out of view and finally disappear in mid-air as it made one last pass over the boat.

Breathing a sigh of relief, they sagged against the rail of the boat and cautiously studied the area around them. For a while all they saw was sunlight and blue water. Thomas was the first to notice anything different.

"Look there," Thomas was suddenly pointing at a speck of land that was becoming visible to the right of the boat.

"Think it's the Island of Hope?" Sara said.

As if in answer to her question, the boat altered its course to head straight for the speck. The alteration brought with it an increased barrage of waves and thumps against the hull of the boat.

"What's that noise?" Fear brought out a squeaking note to James's voice. He moved close to the railing to get a better view of the water. "Look, you guys! There's something down there!"

The teenager squinted, noting a long gray thing floating alongside the hull. Whatever it was bobbed on the waves, bumping against the wood – whack, whack, whack.

"What is that?" James leaned forward in careless fascination.

Sara and Thomas were moving towards him to see what he was looking at when large tentacles snaked up the side of

131

the vessel and grabbed him. Using its strong suction cups, it took hold of James and tried to drag him overboard.

"I believe this is real!" he yelled, hanging onto the railing for dear life, struggling to maintain his grip on the rough spindles.

Splinters embedded themselves into his fingertips. Running to the tentacle that had James in its grasp, Thomas and Sara began to hit it with whatever they could get their hands on. Sara had grabbed a large fishhook from a rack near the cabin and was striking the tentacle as hard as she could. Thankfully, it let go quickly, and James scrambled away toward the cabin, attempting to avoid the other tentacles that continued to slide along the deck. The slimy, thick tubes slithered along the wooden surface, feeling their way towards something. Then failing to make contact again, abruptly stopped their pursuit of James. And then, as if the eyeless pieces of flesh knew exactly where to go, wound their way upward towards the masts, pulling at the sails. The children were forced to dodge falling pieces of wood and thick material as they rained down from the broken rigging.

"Sara, do something!" Thomas cried as they cowered next to the cabin housing, deflecting wood by mentally knocking the larger pieces away from them. Sara tried in vain to use her powers to stir up the waters around the creature. She conjured up images of a whirlpool, hoping to suck the creature down, making it let go of the boat. Unfortunately, once the whirlpool began to form, it also started to pull the boat into it also.

"O.k., stop Sara!" Thomas yelled over the roar of the waves. "That's just making things worse, and that creature's not letting go."

Sara slumped on deck, exhausted from her efforts to control the water. The whirlpool activity stopped and waves crashed against the deck once again. The tentacles continued to wreak havoc on the small boat, breaking off pieces of the railing. Something had to be done soon or there would be no boat left. James pulled his pipe out with shaking hands and began to play. His magical music once again had the desired effect. The boat was released suddenly and fell back into the water with a splash. The tentacles slithered back towards the sea and disappeared into the cold depths. He kept playing until he was out of breath, collapsing against the cabin, waiting for a renewed attack but nothing happened.

Thomas put down the large pole that he had used to poke at the slimy appendages and looked at the island, clearly visible now. The boat was still a good distance from land and bobbing about in the deep water handicapped by the lack of sails now lying about the deck in tatters. In this condition Sara was wondering if the small craft would even be able to make it to their destination. The boat swayed sickeningly in the open sea. There was a hushed expectancy in the air. The only sounds the lapping of the waves against the hull and a gentle breeze blowing all around them. This was not to last, however. The silence was broken by the sound of something heavy hitting the underside of the boat again.

"What now?" said James, getting to his feet.

Thomas and Sara ran to the rail to peer cautiously over the side into the dark water. At first, nothing was visible, then Sara saw something awful. Was that an arm? Squinting to clarify, she continued to stare at the thing in the water. Up from the murky, green sea, popped a pasty white limb – it was indeed an arm with a hand attached at the end. She would have assumed it was something dead but the hand was hitting the hull in a coordinated manner. As she and Thomas watched in horrified fascination, the arm was soon followed by a mass of what appeared to be seaweed attached to a stark white head.

The thing turned toward the boat raising its bloated face skyward. Bright-green eyes stared out from a stark white face, flat nose flared snorting water upward while flat lips stretched to reveal sharp yellowy teeth. Continuing to look on in disbelief, she saw what looked like a scaly tail floating behind the creature.

"Is that supposed to be a mermaid?" Sara said, squinting to get a better look at the thing in the water.

She had seen plenty of pictures of mermaids in books, but they were always pretty creatures with long flowing hair and perfect features. They had pearl necklaces, shell bras, and neat tails attached below their waist. This thing was hideous; its bloated white skin looked like a dead fish she had seen floating on the surface of Hurley Pond last summer. The stringy mass of seaweed on its head appeared to be crawling full of nasty little critters. She couldn't be exactly sure from this distance, but it looked like there were dead fish and maybe some crabs hanging there. As she watched the crabs and sea worms crawling about, Sara had to grab her stomach to keep from hurling. James had joined his friends and together they watched the thing in disbelief. It began to pound its hand against the wooden hull again, hitting it repeatedly. The creature must have had incredible strength because Sara could hear the wood crack and felt the boat lurch as water began to pour into the bottom half of the vessel. The creature looked up at her small audience, puffy white face breaking into a triumphant grin as she dove underwater to finish her destruction of the bottom of the boat.

"Can you get us closer to shore, Sara?" asked Thomas "Water is your specialty. I don't think we're going to last much longer. We're sinking pretty fast."

As if to further illustrate the point, the boat went down lower into the water till the deck was almost at sea level. "And I don't want to be in the water with that thing." James shuddered as he heard another thump and a plank from the hull floated to the surface of the water.

Eager to escape conflict with this very scary thing, she concentrated on the sea behind the boat, creating a wave that rose and pushed them at a faster rate towards the shore. "Brace yourself!" Sara cried as the vessel rushed forwards. Seeking only to protect themselves from impact, they ran towards the cabin and slammed the door behind them. Throwing themselves under the small bed, they held on for dear life as the boat hit the sandy beach with a crash. The impact squished them all against the wall in a tangle of limbs.

The three children crawled clumsily out from underneath the bed and looked each other over to make sure that no one was hurt.

"I'm awfully sorry I stuck my foot in your ribs," Thomas said to James, who was rubbing his side with a pained expression on his face as he struggled to catch his breath. "That's ok," James said. "It couldn't be helped. I'm sorry I elbowed you in the nose" he added, noticing the red mark forming on Thomas's face.

"I'm not entirely sure it was your elbow," Sara said, touching the red mark. "I think it may have been mine. I'm so sorry, you guys. I didn't think we'd make it to shore that fast. I guess I overdid it a bit."

"Well, when it comes to being eaten by a giant squid, coming face to face with that mermaid, or crashing into the sand, I think I'll pick the sand anytime, so don't apologize." James still clutched his sore side.

"Let's check out the damage," Thomas said, leading the way through the cabin which now slanted precariously to the left.

They went out onto the deck and looked around. The boat was indeed leaning to the side, its hull pushed up onto the shore. Pieces of wood were scattered in front of the boat, no doubt part of the bow that had broken off on impact. There were also the gaping holes in the hull caused by their recent visitor.

"I guess we won't be using this boat to leave the island," Sara said, looking back towards the ocean to see a small white blob on the surface. It was the pasty creature who faced them, raising a fist before disappearing beneath the waves.

Shaken, the youngsters walked to the side of the boat closest to the sand and jumped onto the beach at its lowest point. The island was very beautiful with white sandy beaches that met deep blue ocean water. Palm trees grew in abundance alongside banana and coconut trees, each rich with its respective fruit. Colorful birds of every type flew in and around the trees, their exotic songs echoing in the air. They stood silently drinking in all the beautiful sights and enjoying the silence and momentary peace hoping for some kind of sign as to what to do next. "Where do you think Olie is?" Sara peered beyond the trees to check for any buildings where this mysterious and powerful man might be.

"I guess we should go towards the trees," said James, gesturing in that direction. "If I was trying to hide and defend myself from intruders, that's where I'd be."

Not seeing any benefit in standing around, they began to walk that way. All of which seemed to trigger a reaction. As soon as they moved the ground began to shake, and a hot wind blew past their faces.

136

"Here we go again!" Thomas yelled.

A loud roar reverberated throughout the island. The trees in front of them began to part, as if something large were making its way toward them at great speed.

"Real or not real?" Sara said, looking at James and Thomas.

Both boys shrugged their shoulders and waited for the large, scary thing to appear on the beach. And appear it did, in the shape of a large one-eyed giant. The giant towered above the palm trees, uprooting a few of them as he came towards them. It was a terrifying sight, covered in hair from head to foot, its single eye placed high on its forehead. The eye was red and constantly moving as if it had no control of itself. Its massive arms were swinging restlessly around as it pulled up more trees.

"Real or not real?" Sara said again, not sure how to react to this new threat – was it an illusion like the pterodactyl created to scare them off? Or was it a real threat like the thing with the tentacles and the scary mermaids?

"I don't know!" James cried as the giant turned in their direction and began to stomp onto the sand, throwing great drifts of it up all around them.

"Real or not real?" Sara yelled, this time staring at Thomas with a look of desperation. "Not real," Thomas said, suddenly becoming very still, looking behind the giant.

"Ok, then," Sara said. "Think it together. We can only confirm this if we use our connection."

The three of them held hands and repeated over and over again, "Not real, not real, not real…" trying not to react as the giant raced up to them, opened its large mouth, and roared. Sour breath ruffled their hair, and just when they began to think they had been wrong and were about to die, everything stopped and the giant was gone.

The children opened their eyes, which had been closed tightly, and blinked in amazement; they were alone.

"How did you know?" James asked Thomas in amazement, his voice shaky but relieved.

"All of the trees it was busy ripping up still stood behind it, so I figured it had to be an illusion," Thomas said, pointing to the trees in front of them, all planted firmly in the ground.

"Good observation." James patted him on the back. "Where do you think we should go from here, and what other surprises do you think he has in store for us?"

"I'm not sure," Sara said, looking around for a sign that would tell them where to start.

"I think," she started to speak, but stopped abruptly and touched the pocket that she had put the Healing Stone in earlier. She pulled it out and looked closely at it. "This thing is vibrating, and it's getting warm."

She held the stone up in the air and turned to her left; nothing happened. When she turned to her right, the stone glowed a bright red.

"Let's try something," she said, walking toward the right. The stone continued to glow brightly. She turned and began to walk toward the left. The stone stopped glowing and was cold once again.

"I think we're supposed to go that way." She pointed to the right, so they walked in that direction once again, and the stone began to grow warm and bright again.

They walked into the grove of palm trees and followed the directions of the Healing Stone. Changing direction as the color changed, they paid little attention to their surroundings other than to note that they were in a jungle now. They heard the sounds of birds calling to one another and what might have been the distant cry of a big cat. The air around them was now growing humid. The children began to sweat profusely in their borrowed clothes. The long-sleeved shirts and pants had provided a little protection in the Cold Caverns, but were becoming uncomfortable in the heat. But at least the clothing kept the mosquitoes from stinging too much exposed skin. As it was, they were slapping constantly at their necks and hands to ward off the frequent blood raids. The Healing Stone was glowing brighter now with each step they took, so encouraged, they continued on.

"We must be getting very close now," Sara observed. "This stone is getting awfully warm."

Thomas and James looked at the stone as Sara held it up. It was indeed glowing like a bright red laser, easily visible even in the sunlit area they were now standing in. The stone had their full attention and almost caused them to bump into an object they had not previously noticed. They stopped in front of a flat stone rock formation that seemed to rise up out of nowhere in the middle of the dense undergrowth they had been walking through. Chalky white and huge, it towered above them about fifty feet straight up. There were strange symbols carved in the rock wall, leaves: tall, thin figures with distorted faces, a diamond shape, which looked a little like the stone she was holding, and a half moon shape that looked like the mark the three of them shared.

At the bottom of the rock was a small opening shaped like a half-moon. It was toward this opening that they had begun to move when the previously quiet area was disturbed by the sound of chirping and croaking, like a million creatures had suddenly been set loose. Startled, they looked up to find that the trees around them were suddenly filled with brightly colored frogs, some blue with green spots, some red with dark spots, some small, some large. As if on command, the frogs were jumping down from the trees and crawling to the children at a fast pace.

"Wow, cool-looking frogs!" James said, looking more closely as the frogs approached.

"Cool-looking poisonous frogs!" Sara said as she recognized the animals from her studies in science class. Though very pretty, she had learned their skin was coated with a deadly, harmful substance. The fact had fascinated her, that such a small being had the power to protect itself from other creatures. In her previous situation she'd wished for the ability to protect herself, too, maybe not that way, but with enough power to drive the bad people away. Her admiration for that particular skill was not as high at this particular moment – as it looked as if it was intended to be used against them.

"If we come in contact with their skin, it can be very bad. Some of the poisons can kill shortly after contact."

"And it looks as if they want to make contact," Thomas observed as they inched closer together. To protect themselves, the children stood back to back and held hands once again. Thomas concentrated on lifting the frogs and sending them flying back towards the trees, but another power was working against him, and the frogs, rather than hitting the trees, hit an invisible barrier, bouncing back towards them in larger numbers than before. The air filled with the chirping and croaking sounds of thousands of bright frogs quickly converging on the helpless youngsters. James tried to move his hands to reach for his flute but Sara would not release her grip. Driven by an impulse to not break contact with her companions, she turned and shook her head at him. Feeling her certainty about maintaining contact, he gave in and allowed her to continue holding his hand.

"But how are we supposed to protect ourselves?" James felt compelled to ask as the frogs came closer still.

The answer came from the stone itself. It began to glow even brighter in Sara's hand as she pressed it to James's. The glow spread out all around them. The frogs retreated. The narrow doorway in the stone widened as if in welcome, and a feeling of great well-being worked its way through the children.

"I think he knows now who is here," Sara said as the noise around them stopped and they felt secure enough to let go of each other's hands. "I don't know if he recognizes us or the stone, but I think we've been given permission to proceed without any other problems."

As if to confirm her theory, the opening in the stone widened even further and a light came from the opening as if to guide them in.

"Ok, Olie, we're coming, but please play nice," Sara said as they moved to the opening and walked inside.

Chapter Eighteen

The awe-filled friends walked slowly into a brightly lit area with walls of gleaming white stone. A cool breeze circulating in the large chamber from holes located high overhead, created a comfortable atmosphere. A golden light came from within the walls around them illuminating the area with crystal clarity. The smooth stone was highly polished and so beautiful it took Sara's breath away. The longer she looked at the wall, the more she thought she saw things she couldn't possibly see. Indistinct images flickered teasingly over the surface. She had the irresistible urge to get a closer look. The images became clearer as she approached – smiling people, laughing babies, people holding out their hands towards her with looks of compassion and complete love. It was like watching a greeting card commercial, but so much more, because it triggered emotions far beyond the soppy sentimentality they were intended to conjure. It was as if they had tapped into her innermost thoughts, conveying an understanding of who she was, drawing her in with the unconditional love she had always wanted.

Unable to resist the impulse, she lifted a hand in response to the beckoning figures in front of her, as if she could touch the people she saw. Of all the figures present, she felt particularly drawn to an image of a tall, fair-haired couple who were smiling at her so lovingly that it made her heart ache to see them. All other forms faded away until they stood face to face, their lips moved but no sound came out. She leaned forward as far as she could without bumping her nose into the wall,

Sara jumped back, startled to feel Thomas's hand on her shoulder. He too, was closely studying the wall in front of her an amazed expression on his face.

"What do you see?" she asked curiously, watching his eyes tear over as if something deeply moved him.

"I think I see my real mother and father," he said, crying openly now. "I feel that they're here somehow."

James moved towards the wall as if drawn there by what he saw.

"Yes, I think they are," he said, reaching for the wall to touch it gently.

They stood there for a long time, entranced by the images of their parents, before reluctantly turning away. The scenes didn't change and they were unable to make contact with them. It was a running loop of some kind, nothing more, another distraction to keep them at bay.

"We have to find Olie," Sara said. "He's hurt, remember? He's the key to all of this, and if we want to make things right, make our parents' sacrifice worth it. We have to help him and ask him what we need to do." She turned reluctantly from the wall and walked down the long, thin hallway in front of her.

As they progressed, the light seemed to get brighter, both from the walls around her and the Healing Stone. It shone so intensely now it almost blinded her. She barely saw the small opening at the end of the hallway, stepping through it caused the lights to return to the soft glow that had been there before. She was in a small room now, with a stone bed in the center. On the bed was a large man with dark hair. His eyes were closed and his breaths no more than shallow gasps, as if he was in a great deal of pain. She looked him over carefully, but was not able to find any source of injury. Placing her hand gently on his arm, she shook him to get a response; there was none. He simply lay there pale and looking very uncomfortable. Sara felt the presence of the boys in the room behind her, but did not turn around.

"Why won't he wake up?"

Thomas had moved up behind her to look at the man. Shaking what he assumed was the man named Olie's arm, he got the same response – none.

"I don't know. I'm not a doctor. He just looks like he's sleeping." Sara stated the obvious.

"Do you think music would help?" James raised his flute but Sara stopped him.

"Not sure," she replied. "Let's wait. I didn't know he was like this. How could he have given us so much grief on the way here if he was like this?"

Sara shrugged and waited for something magical to happen, and it was then the Healing Stone made its purpose known. It went from a muted pink color to bright-red, the comforting warmth began to rise. The hand holding the stone moved of its own accord. Propelled by a vibration from within, it jerked up, her fingers making contact with Olie's until it was clear that the stone belonged in his hand. Obeying the object, she carefully placed the Healing Stone in the man's hand and backed away. Instantly, there was a warm red glow that spread over his body, and his pale skin began to take on a rosy glow. His breathing became more relaxed, and his eyes opened. They were the most beautiful eyes she had ever seen. Dark and deep, they held at once laughter and profound compassion, and when they focused on her, she felt complete peace and love.

Olie raised himself up from the bed and smiled at the three children as if he'd been expecting them. His next statement confirmed this.

"I have been waiting for you to come," he said in a voice so soothing that Sara couldn't help but smile. "It's so good to have both new and old friends with me again. Shalsar dwells within you." He looked at Sara. "She was such a wonderful guardian. She had command of all the bodies of water in this land. She is a wonderful soul, and I know she is honored to share her powers with a brave and resourceful girl such as you are, Sara." He bowed deeply as he spoke, pretending he did not see her looking at him with her mouth wide open in shock.

He then addressed her companions. "It is my honor to make your acquaintance. Thomas, you are a worthy companion to Marthon. He was a guardian of many talents. His powers of observation were wondrous, and ability to control objects from afar was amazing. He was with me till the very end of my battle with the Garren's strongest forces. He fought so hard to save me. I sense that you are not as strong as he was yet, but will be soon."

Olie then approached James and patted him on the back. "I am proud to meet you, James. Argus is positively beaming through you. He is showing me that he has had such a good life with you. He has so much more to share; his power of music is only the beginning. He also has the power to mesmerize in other ways, too. He has so much he can teach you. You are such an extraordinary young man." Olie moved away and continued to address the children like the old friends he was convinced they were carrying inside of them. But, in typical Keeper manner, he spent little time in this sentimental pursuit and got straight to the point.

"I know that your journey has been difficult and dangerous, and I wish I could let you rest, but we must act soon if we are to defeat our enemies. In the first battle with the Garren, I was overwhelmed by the level of their hatred. Foolishly I assumed that people's reaction to being exposed to all that evil would be to fight harder to overcome it, but I was wrong. Most gave in easily. Then I thought that I could make it all go away, but it takes more time with some than with others. It was the few that I tried hardest to heal that turned on me, almost killing me. The hatred placed by the Garren was stronger than common sense or love. I had to pull back and close down till my powers could be restored to full strength. I was waiting for the Healing Stone and the right people to bring it to me."

He held up the glowing red gem. "Now, we must go aid the Keepers in their fight. They are valiantly battling to keep the Garren from reaching us. I must protect my people and show them that there is hope. The greatest soul of all will be there to help; it is from him that we gather strength. Follow me. We must go to the fight."

Without explaining to whom he referred, Olie walked towards the entrance and out into the warm sunshine. Once outside, he raised his arms to the sky, and the air was filled with a soft humming sound like the fluttering of many wings. The bewildered group looked up to find that there were several large moths hovering in the sky above them. The moths were beautiful, with large green wings, distinct eye-shaped patterns in the center, and a light tracing of pink on the outer edges. Sara thought they looked like the Luna Silk Moths she had studied in science class, only twenty times larger than any of the specimens she had seen and big enough to sit on. And it looked as if that's what they were about to do, as the moths glided down to the ground at Olie's command. Showing them how easy it was, he gently climbed on the moth's back and gestured for the children to do the same. With little hesitation, the children climbed aboard. It was a slightly better seat than the spider's back, the wings were smooth to the touch and furry bodies were not as stiff as spider hair.

Excited to have such a luxurious ride, Sara held on to the moth's warm, fuzzy center as it wriggled around in preparation for flight. She looked over at the two boys as they took seats on the large moths. They had looks of complete joy on their faces. If anything happened during this flight, that was exactly how she wanted to remember her friends; happy just like this. Passengers safely settled, the moths scrambled across the ground and flapped their wings vigorously to rise into the air. The view from the sky was beautiful. They were high enough to see the tops of palm trees as they swayed in the breeze. The light was rapidly fading, and the sunset was a wonderful mixture of red and gold in the western sky. The cool night breeze blew past Sara's face as they sped into the night to help the Keepers.

Their journey was a long and uneventful, the silence only broken by the occasional ooohs and aaahhhs let out by the children as they flew through the sky.

As night settled over the land, the stars sparkled against the dark velvety sky like diamonds. It was a view that Sara vowed she would never forget. Soon they were fast approaching the shore where they had last seen the Keepers. They could see a struggle going on down below. The moths dipped lower to get a better look at the action on the beach. They could see flashes of light followed by shrill screams of pain. Darkly clothed figures were running into the trees, only to emerge a short while later and hover uncertainly on the beach. At the shoreline stood a long line of brightly clothed Keepers. The dark figures shrank back and seemed reluctant to go toward the light the Keepers were shining at them. *The Keepers are winning!* Sara thought as she watched the battle. Once again, the dark clothed army fell back to the trees. She was smiling, cheering them on inside, hoping they could just land and it would be all over, hoping the doubt that was beginning to build in her gut was wrong and what she was seeing was the real and final result, of the Keepers being more powerful than those they fought. Then, suddenly, her

148

internal fears were confirmed. Instead of the dark figures they'd seen before, a large group of tall, skinny creatures appeared from the forest. With their long, clumsy limbs, they looked like stick men on stilts, yet moved gracefully and with great speed as they ran towards the Keepers. The tall men pointed at the Keepers, and a dark, fine mist appeared in the air. Then sadly, the Keepers began to fall back in the presence of the mist. The glowing heroes were moving towards the sea, batting wildly at the air around their bodies. Some fell to the ground while others tried to rally and continue their assault with the light.

Unfortunately, the Keepers light didn't seem to have much effect on the dark men, who simply kept walking toward them unaffected.

"The Garren have come," said Olie, pointing to the dark men. "Now is our time to enter the battle."

Olie directed his moth down toward the shore, and the others followed after him, turning abruptly to dive at the Garren as they advanced on the Keepers.

"Join with me!" Olie cried as the moths landed on the sand. Not having the time or choice to do otherwise, the children scrambled off their mounts and ran to Olie, joining hands with him. They had landed directly in front of the Garren as they pursued the Keepers, and Sara was startled to find herself face to face with the creatures that she had been running from for so long. Finally, the enemy had a face, a stark white, emotionless face. There wasn't even a glimmer of surprise at the sudden appearance of Olie and the children on the beach. Long, dark hair hung over pasty, withered faces with no variation in features, they were looking at the same person multiplied many times and everything about them appeared cold and empty. It was like looking at a moving shell of flesh: there was substance outside, but nothing present inside. The Garren were just puppets bent on completing a task, and that task was to destroy the Keepers. The icy grey eyes of the enemy looked through them as they continued to walk toward the Keepers, not even pausing at their arrival in the path of attack. Sara felt a buzzing in her head as she watched the evil creatures speed towards them, an enormous pressure built up in her head and drove her to her knees. Clutching her head with both hands, she struggled to regain her footing, fighting the nausea caused by her movements. She turned her head slightly and saw her companions go down one by one. *This can't be happening*, she cried out in her mind. *We have come so far. They can't win; we can't let them.*

Sara turned her head to see that while the rest of the group was writhing around on the ground, Olie was still standing. He looked directly at her and she felt the urge to get up despite the intense pressure in her head, and she forced her wobbly legs to straighten. Her companions were also on their feet now. Olie was holding the group together, fighting off the evil with his will, and as she watched, he raised his arm and reached for her hand. As Sara grasped Olie's hand, she felt the now familiar warmth sweep through her. Thomas quickly grabbed her other hand, then James's. The Healing Stone began to glow brightly around them, and continued to glow brighter and brighter as the Garren approached. In addition to the red glow of the Healing Stone, Sara noticed that a brighter light from above them had joined with their own. They were glowing so intensely now they were nearly transparent. She later found out from Olie that this light was called Iam, and he was the true power above them all, the one he had been referring to before. The Garren closest to their group finally reached the light surrounding them. As it shone on him, he faltered and fell to his knees. Temporarily stunned by the power in the air, he was unable to move even an inch further. Then, to Sara's amazement, she saw tears appear in the creature's eyes. He reached a pale, bony hand to his face and touched the moisture on his cheeks. The Garren's face turned upwards towards the bright light, and she saw his lips form what may have been a pained attempt to smile, to perform that long unused function.

The enemy looked at them as if noticing their presence at last, and with hands limply at his sides, sat quietly in the sand and continued to cry. The light had the same effect on all the Garren it touched, and soon there were a great number of them sitting in a line on the sand, silently crying. A few of the Garren had turned aside at the last moment to flee back into the woods and disappear before reaching the light. Sara was not sure what had prompted them to do so. For the most part, however, the Garren seemed to have been deeply affected by the presence of their combined powers and that of Iam above them. The change was remarkable. The longer Sara looked at the Garren, the less pasty their faces became. They were now glowing with an inner light, which softened their features and brought an animated quality to them. Previously cold, grey eyes were now glowing with joy, and were looking at everything around them with the wonder of little children.

Olie gently squeezed Sara's hand and released it at the same time he let go of the boys. The glow around them subsided, but the Garren sat still on the ground, happy to remain, experiencing emotion. Sara felt the presence of the other Keepers as they approached from behind, each of them expressing their gratitude for the sudden rescue. They hugged each of the children and greeted Olie with affection and respect. Sara stood among them, content to just absorb the happiness of the moment. She knew that there were a few things for them to do before this was all over. It seemed too easy to have ended like this. But was it really over? And what did this mean for her if it was?

Chapter Nineteen

The next few months, Olie and the children traveled extensively, healing all the people affected by the hatred that spread over the land. Most people were easy. They were glad to be healed but there were a few people who resisted. Olie had to try harder to banish the hatred from them. Some were healed only after a long fight, grudgingly accepting assistance when it could no longer be avoided. Unfortunately, there were others who ran away rather than be healed, preferring for some strange reason to pledge themselves to the darkness of a hopeless life. Whatever the Garren had offered them must have been very powerful for them to reject what the Keepers could do for them. Sara had heard that the runners had joined with the small group of the Garren who had escaped during the battle with the Keepers. Together they were hiding on another island far from this one. Olie chose not to pursue them at this time, concentrating instead on all those he could help. Saying only that he knew they'd have to face them again.

"It was inevitable," he'd said, leaving Sara to ponder his ominous tone and wonder why he looked so sad.

During their travels through the land, the children had helped cure many people. Sara, Thomas, and James worked tirelessly with Olie to reach every region that the Garren had been. Sara felt good about all that they had done, felt such joy every time they helped a person come back from the hatred. Having traveled to many places, it was quite some time before they returned to the town where James and his family had lived. The group stopped at Uncle Tim's house first. James was overjoyed to see that his brothers and sisters were all safe and untouched by the hatred. Uncle Tim said that a group of the Garren's scouts had tried to get to them, and he'd given them quite the fight, but, for some unknown reason, when they made it to the top of the tree, they stopped suddenly and ran away.

"That must have been the same time as the battle, when a large number of them advanced to our area," James said as he hugged his brothers and sisters and told them all about the adventures he'd had while he was away.

"I am so glad you're alright. I wish I'd been there to help you. Are you going to find your parents now?" Uncle Tim asked gently, noting the faraway look on James's face and the way he kept looking towards the town.

"Yes, I have to find them. I have to see if they're okay," said James, fearing the worst had happened already.

"Then I will go with you," vowed Uncle Tim. "Two of the Keepers have offered to stay with the children. Patrick and Ella need us." He put his arm around James's shoulders, and after assuring the children they would return with their parents, they turned and walked towards Sara and the others.

As they neared the town, they could see the damage that had been done since they had last been there. Trees were hacked down where before they had been growing plentifully. What had been a lovely, well-kept town was now in ruins. The streets were filled with litter, and the well-tended houses were falling apart. Shutters were hanging on by one hinge, and jagged pieces of glass hung from the many broken windows they passed on their way to James's house. The pleasant, well stocked shops Sara remembered were empty, display cases torn out, and smashed in the street in pieces. People were wandering aimlessly around with blank, fixed stares. The only change in their appearance occurred when they saw Olie and the others, and turned towards them with open dislike on their faces. It hurt Sara to see the curled lips and furrowed brows directed at her, especially on the faces of small children. It was that same look that she had gotten all those years while living with the Finklesteins. It still hurt just as much now as it did then. Olie looked at her as if he knew what she was thinking, and he smiled at her reassuringly. He held out his hand and they drifted past raised fists and savage kicks aimed but failing to make contact, bravely letting their combined powers work with the Healing Stone.

A bright golden red light shown from them, keeping back the most violent, until all were bathed in the glow, stopping all activity as the poison was sucked from their minds and they became normal people again. Faces first bewildered then smiling from ear to ear, surrounded them, this time with hugs and many thank you's.

Caught up in the moment, Sara was smiling brightly and laughing with the newly healed townspeople. Then she looked at James and her smile faded. James was looking about the town anxiously, obviously searching for his parents. Tears were forming in his eyes as he failed to find them in the crowd. He turned towards his house and began to run as fast as he could.

Sara ran along with him, not willing to let him face whatever he found there alone. When they sighted the house, it looked nothing like the homely place they'd left. The windows were boarded up on the outside, but some of the wooden planks had been torn away, with enough force to bend the metal nails backwards, leaving them poking out one side, like spiked weapons left strewn about the ground. Slowing her pace, Sara carefully navigated her way past them, but was troubled to see some kind of sticky red substance on the end of a few nails, together with what might have been hair. But even worse, on the front of the house, in yet more sticky red liquid, written in large letters was WHERE ARE THEY? On the stony, blood-soaked ground were thick sticks and piles of stones, broken dishes and few thick bronze statues that she thought she'd recognized as having been in the living room of James's house. The top windows had been opened and Sara could see more projectiles sitting upon the window-ledge as if someone had been launching them from this last safe place at whoever had initiated the attack upon their abode.

With heavy hearts, they moved closer noting that the front door had been knocked off its hinges, and lay on the front steps broken in pieces. The inside of the house was a wreck: tables were overturned and all the contents of the cabinets were emptied out on the floor in a messy heap. "Father? Mother?" James's called out in a broken yet hopeful voice.

Whoever had done this damage had been looking for him and Sara. It was obvious that they were the subject of the message on the front of the house, since it was not written anywhere else. And those attackers had been filled with rage. There was blood everywhere. It looked as if whatever had happened, James's parents had put up quite a struggle. *Please don't let the blood be theirs.*

As they crossed the threshold, Sara and James stared at each other with that thought swimming between them. At first glance, there was no one in the house, but then Sara heard a rustling noise coming from the room to the left of the front entrance. Cautiously, she walked towards the sound completely ignoring James's cautionary message from somewhere behind her. There was a sudden movement as something scurried past the open doorway and settled behind a pile of broken furniture in the corner. Her breath caught in her throat as she saw a large, pale hand reach out from behind the pile and grab a broken table leg. Then, without another sound, Mr. Marsden rose and rushed at her with the table leg in his raised hand ready to strike. He had a crazed look of pure hatred on his face. His bright-red hair stood out at all angles, and it looked as if he had not shaved in weeks. Lips curled in rage, he swung the wooden leg at her. Quickly she moved to the side and felt the rush of air as the club just missed her head. Panicked, Sara threw herself behind the remains of what had been the kitchen table. Pulling up a large plank of wood torn from the center, she cowered behind it, using it as an improvised shield. Worried now that James was unprotected, she tried to keep his father's focus on her until he could bring Olie back. In her head, she was already throwing out instructions to go for help when she felt the impact of the table leg slamming into the wood.

"Mr. Marsden!" she screamed, "Please, don't, it's me, Sara. We're here to help you."

Her arm ached from the blow to her shield. She was shaking uncontrollably to think that such a good man could act this way. At that moment, there was nothing of the jovial family man that she had met months earlier.

There was a brief pause in the assault, as Mr. Marsden raised the club again, and she took this opportunity to scramble backwards and hide herself behind a stuffed armchair. She heard his heavy footsteps follow, and the chair was roughly pushed aside. The club was raised again. Hoping James had managed to get far enough away to avoid seeing what came next, Sara raised her arms in anticipation of the forthcoming blow. The silence was broken by the sound of James's flute. Mr. Marsden stopped and slowly turned towards him. Transfixed by the soothing music, he was looking at James in amazement; shaking his head several times, as if to clear it, while slowly lowering the table leg. For a moment, he stood still, then raised his hand and held it out to James. There was complete despair in the man's eyes, as if he was now aware of his actions, but still could not stop himself. The music was only a temporary reprieve. They needed to act quickly before its spell diminished. As James lowered his flute and took his father's hand, she was dismayed to see that same large hand close in a crushing grip as soon as the music faded away. Fearing for James's safety, Sara quickly grabbed his hand. As she did so, she felt her other hand grabbed by Olie, who was suddenly standing behind her, with Thomas at his side. It was then the room took on the bright-red glow of the Healing Stone. They stood together caught up in the magic and power ebbing and flowing over them. Soon James was embracing his smiling father, who, in turn, was hugged affectionately by his brother, Tim.

After a brief conversation, Mr. Marsden lead them to his wife, who he'd hidden in the tunnel and had been given strict instructions not to allow anyone in. It was just as they'd suspected. The affected townsfolk had visited the house demanding that he turn over the blonde girl and the boy they knew was not really his son.

"They'd known us for years and had never talked about James as anything but mine. But now it was like they'd been told who to look for. We were no longer their neighbors, we were their enemy. And it wasn't just them. There were some funny-looking monkey people trying to climb the walls. Mom and I took out a few of them by throwing heavy things out of the window before I made sure she hid in the cellar."

As he spoke he patted his wife's back, a look of pride on his face that she'd done so much to help but also that he'd been able to protect her from the worst of the attack.

"When they made it through, I fought them with all I had, but it was hard to see people I respected trying to hurt me…" Mr. Marsden stopped for a moment and let out a breath trying to regain his composure. "I didn't have the heart to kill them. And I don't think they wanted to kill me, more like find out what I knew about where you two were." He nodded to Sara and James. "And then some tall skinny men came in and there was this black mist. I don't remember anything after that."

For her part, Mrs. Marsden was happy to have her husband and son back with her. When she was told that her other children were safe, she was anxious to get to them. James left with his family to go to his brothers and sisters. Sara stayed behind with Olie and Thomas, feeling suddenly apprehensive now that their job appeared to be done. The one thing both she and Thomas seemed to have in common was the fact that they had no one to go home to, and where, in fact, not sure where home would be. Sara was hoping she could stay with James's family, but was beginning to get the sinking feeling that wasn't going to be up to her.

"Thomas, I have to tell you, we have looked all over the land for your parents, and we have been unable to find them." Olie patted Thomas's hand as the boy bowed his head in sorrow.

"We will continue to look, of course, but I would like for you to stay with me and learn to develop your talents."

Thomas nodded his head and asked hopefully. "You will continue to look, though, right?"

"Yes, we will," Olie assured him.

"Then I will stay with you, until we find them," Thomas said confidently.

She knew he felt this would be a short-term situation and would soon be back with his parents. Sara hoped he was right.

"I would be honored to have you in my life," Olie said earnestly.

Thomas smiled and looked at Sara. "What about Sara? You don't intend for her to go back with the Finklesteins, do you?"

"No. Sara is very important to us," said Olie, looking at her with his kind, dark eyes. "You have endured far more than any of the others, long before this even began, yet you remained untouched by the hatred around you. You are the strongest of them all. You just don't realize it yet. Shalsar's spirit survived because of you. She shows me how you rose above it all and did not allow your spirits to fall into despair. You shined despite what was given to you in life, and that is true power. As with the others, you have many gifts that are not developed at this time. They will come to light later. In the meantime, we owe it to you to provide you with a comforting and loving place to develop your talents. I must explain to you that, given the situation, with the evil Garren still roaming around, it is not safe for all of you to be together. I do not think you should remain in this world. You must remain in the world that you came from. But you will have a Keeper to accompany you. Rianna has asked that she be given the honor of going with you. She knows what you can be, and wants to help you lead a happy life until your destiny can be fulfilled."

"I thought this was my destiny, to accomplish what we have just accomplished," Sara said with a sigh.

"No, dear. Your life will be incredibly full and rich, but there is more to this struggle than you realize. Rianna can teach you the history of the Keepers and what we were made for. She will be good for you," Olie told her with absolute conviction.

Sara sat for a moment and thought about what Olie had just said. She could not think of anything that was worth returning to in her former life. It had to be better this time.

160

She nodded at Olie and said, "I would like that very much." And she turned at a sound in the doorway behind her. There was Rianna, smiling at her and holding out her hand. Sara stood up and took her hand. She was startled to see that the woman's gray hair had turned golden blonde, and the years seemed to melt away from her face. A pretty thirty-year old lady was smiling at her and pulling her into a brightly lit doorway. Without getting a chance to say goodbye, she crossed the threshold with Rianna and found that they were suddenly standing in front of a lovely house with a lush green lawn. A large golden retriever barked in greeting as they walked through the front door, and a black cat curled around her ankles, purring an affectionate welcome as if she'd known and loved her for a long time. Sara smiled. This was something she could get used to: a real home filled with love.

And so, it was as she expected, settling in, making friends, and starting her life as an ordinary child in an ordinary world, never having to look back at where she had been, well maybe once…

A few months into her new life, on a lazy Sunday morning, Sara was reading the paper at the kitchen table, when she noticed the headline,

PROMINENT COUPLE CONVICTED OF FRAUD.

She continued to read the article with interest:

Wealthy socialites, Hugh and Janet Finklestein, have been convicted of many counts of land and internet fraud after months of investigation by federal authorities. The investigation into the couple's activities began after reports of the mysterious disappearance of the couple's adopted child, Sara. The disappearance was reported by several of the child's teachers and acquaintances after she had failed to show up for her regular activities. Thankfully, the girl was found to be safe and sound and has now been adopted by a suitable guardian after it was determined that the Finklesteins adoption was not legal. The couple admitted to falsifying the paperwork after a tall, gangly man approached them and offered them a large sum of money to keep the infant in their home. Once authorities began looking into the couple's past, they found many interesting facts about their business practices.

After the couple's conviction, their property was seized and sold to pay back the many victims of their illegal scams.

The couple's two children, Amy and Andy, have been sent to live with distant relatives who will raise them with strict discipline and a loving hand, stated Judge Horrace 'Ferd' Jefferson, the presiding judge on this case.

Sara stopped reading the article and looked at Rianna, who was smiling at her from across the table.

"Things do even out in the end, do they not?" Rianna said pleasantly.

"I do believe you are right," Sara replied. "A very wise man once told me that very thing."

Laughing, they finished their breakfast and prepared for another wonderful day together.

THE END OF THE BEGINNING